Winter's Crimes 16

WINTER'S CRIMES

16

edited by Hilary Hale

St. Martin's Press
New York

The stories are copyright respectively:

The Party of the Second Part. Copyright © 1984 by Ted Allbeury
Don't Know Much About Art. Copyright © 1984 by Simon Brett
I Do Dwell. Copyright © 1984 by Lionel Davidson
A Very Special Relationship. Copyright © 1984 by Michael Gilbert
The Reluctant Detective. Copyright © 1984 by Michael Z. Lewin
Remember That Joke, Harry? Copyright © 1984 by Sabensa Gakulu Limited
Come To Dust. Copyright © 1984 by Ellis Peters
Form. Copyright © 1984 by Miles Tripp
The Bully. Copyright © 1984 by David Williams

ISBN 0-312-88243-2

First published in Great Britain by Macmillan London Limited

First U.S. edition 1984

10 9 8 7 6 5 4 3 2 1

CONTENTS

Editor's Note

The sixteenth volume of *Winter's Crimes* continues the tradition established by George Hardinge of containing stories especially written for the collection.

I would like to thank the distinguished contributors for their support in creating a collection of stories which covers nearly every aspect of the genre: from murder to robbery to fraud. Perhaps the only common denominator in the book is the high quality and inventiveness of the writing.

Hilary Hale

Ted Allbeury

THE PARTY OF THE SECOND PART

Brewster had been managing clerk for the chambers ever since he came back from the war. He knew the skills and vagaries of his principals like a farmer knows his dairy herd. When he knocked on the door marked Mathew Porter he stepped into the QC's office with the brief held firmly in his hand. The lawyer was scribbling notes on his pad, one hand keeping open one of the bound Law Reports for 1938. He glanced up at Brewster and pointed to a space on his desk with his gold pencil.

'Stick it down there, Brewster, please.'

'I thought I'd better have a word with you about it, sir. It's from Mr Maclean.'

'What is it?'

'Defence of a divorce petition.'

Porter shook his head. 'You know I never do Family Court cases. Give it to Mr Henry.'

'Mr Maclean insisted it should be you, sir.'

'He ought to know better, he's been dealing with us for long enough.'

'Quite, sir. He gives the chambers a lot of work. That's why I hesitated to refuse the brief. But he says you'd understand when you'd perused it.'

Porter leaned back in his chair looking at Brewster. 'Don't use words like peruse to me, Brewster. You sound like a City of London copper first time in court. I don't peruse the bloody things. I read 'em.'

'It was Mr Maclean's word, sir.'

Porter laughed. 'OK, I'll have a look at it, but you'll have to pass it over to our Henry.' He paused and reached for a pack of Gauloise. 'Why does he want me to take it?'

'The party was in Special Operations Executive during the war. That was your mob wasn't it, sir?'

Porter raised his eyebrows. 'Leave it with me. I'll talk to Maclean myself when I've read it.'

'Right you are, sir.'

'What's the defendant's name by the way?' He leaned forward and looked at the brief. It said Pryke *v* Pryke. 'Pryke. I don't recognise the name. Was he in the French Section?'

'No idea, sir. It's not a chap, it's a woman.'

'OK. Leave it with me.'

Mathew Porter read through the brief and agreed to have lunch with Maclean at the Law Society. They were neither of them great social chatterers and Porter got down to business as soon as they had ordered.

'I wanted to have a word with you about that Pryke brief. It's not my kind of thing you know, Jamie. I never do divorces. Why not let Henry take it over? He's the expert.'

Maclean smiled. 'Have you read the brief?'

'Of course.'

'What did you think of it?'

'Not a cat in hell's chance. Can't see why she's defending it. If her husband can substantiate half what he alleges she's wasting her time and ours. And her money too.'

'She's got a fantastic war record, Mathew. OBE and Legion of Honour from the French. I thought you might have a fellow feeling. Comrades in arms and all that.'

'I say, this soup is terribly salty . . . comrades in arms you say.' He paused with the spoon raised to his lips. 'You know SOE wasn't like a regiment. Too dispersed. Loyalties were very local and personal.' He sighed. 'Apart from all that they were a very mixed bunch. Couldn't say that there were more than

12

half a dozen I'd like to see again. Who's been briefed for the other side?'

'Lowther. Sir Geoffrey himself.'

'Why the big guns? I'd have thought the plaintiff would sail through this. Why the hell does she want to defend anyway?'

'Two reasons, I think. First she doesn't believe in divorce and secondly she was staggered at the stuff they were using against her.'

'What's she like?'

'A nice woman. Quiet, but plenty of guts. Intelligent and well-educated. And quite attractive.'

'I'd have advised her to cut her losses. Call it a day.' He smiled. 'Plenty of other fish in the sea and all that.'

'I feel she's being put upon, Mathew. Blackmailed almost.'

'How do you make that out?'

'I think I could have persuaded her to let it go through, until she saw the other side's accusations. That really put her hackles up. And the husband's a poor specimen anyway.'

'Why do you say that?'

'No decent chap would want to throw this sort of muck at a woman like her. She doesn't deserve it, believe me.'

Porter smiled. 'Sounds like you've got a soft spot for her, Jamie.'

'I have. She was a heroine and she's being abused for it.'

'Was the husband in the services during the war?'

'No. He was some minor civil servant at the War Office. That's how he met her. He was her escort to the Palace when she was presented with her medal. Fell madly in love with her. Swept her off her feet, and now he turns on her.' He dabbed his lips with a paper napkin. 'I thought I might persuade you to put up a bit of a fight on her behalf. As things are she'll lose but she deserves a helping hand.'

'All anybody can do is make the other side look as unpleasant as they really are. Henry could do that better than I can. I'm not much of an advocate. Industrial courts don't like advocates. Just precedents.'

13

'Would you have a word with her? Just a quick conference. For me, Mathew.'

Porter smiled. 'Of course I will, Jamie.How about you send her over to me tomorrow about three?'

Maclean smiled. 'I won't forget it. Thanks.'

'You said just now – "as things stand she'll lose". What did you mean?'

'Did I say that? Well, I shouldn't have. Talking out of turn.'

'Come on. Out with it.'

'You won't mention this to her will you?'

'Not if you say I shouldn't.'

'She knows something about him that could knock his whole case down. The real reason why he wants the marriage finished. She won't let me use it. Made me promise.'

'Do you know what it is?'

'Yes.'

'Tell me.'

'I can't. I promised. I did a bit of rooting around on this fellow Pryke and came across this . . . fact . . . let's call it. I told her about it but she already knew. Flew off the handle at me for being a busybody. Said that using it would make her no better than him. She's right of course, but by God *I'd* have used it.'

'Give me a clue.'

'Don't tempt me, Mathew.'

Porter laughed. 'An indirect clue.'

For a few moments Maclean sat silent and then he opened his mouth to speak, hesitated and then closed his mouth. Porter waited. Then Maclean said, 'Think of the reasons why he might not have been called up in the war.'

Porter shrugged. 'I'll think about it. Tomorrow at three.'

She wasn't at all what Porter had expected. She was prettier. Forty-ish, but with one of those faces whose bone-structure would always make her look younger than her years. She wore a summer dress that gave her an almost schoolgirlish air of innocence. The grey-blue eyes looked at him calmly, but the tension showed in her tight-clasped hands.

He didn't refer to her husband's statement, but talked about what she hoped for by defending the action.

She shrugged. 'I'd just like somebody who believes in me to make me seem less of a . . . harridan . . . than they're trying to make me out.'

'I could call people from SOE or their records to establish that you were very brave and operated in enemy-occupied territory.'

'I wouldn't want them dragged in. The publicity will be bad enough whatever I say. And I don't want to pose as a heroine.'

'But you were.'

She laughed softly. 'You were in SOE, so you know better than that. The heroines were burnt in the ovens at Mauthausen and Ravensbruck.'

'You didn't get an OBE for sitting around in the Dordogne.'

She shook her head. 'The things I did were done in desperation. I'm a natural born coward, not a heroine.'

'Mr Maclean asked me to take the brief, but I must point out that I'm not a divorce lawyer and that could be to your disadvantage.'

'I'd still be grateful if you took it on.'

'Why?'

'Because you were in SOE and I'll know that there's one other person in court who knows what it was all about.' She smiled. 'Somebody to wear my lace hankie on his lance.'

Porter smiled and stood up. 'All right. On your head be it. I'll phone Jamie Maclean and tell him I'll act for you.'

She was trembling as he walked her to the outer office and he went back to his own office and picked up the phone.

'Get me Colonel Ramage, please. His number's in our book. It might be under War Office Records or the Military Secretary's office . . . thank you.'

15

Standing in the court corridors always lowered clients' morale and he took her down to the canteen until they were called.

She was wearing a pale blue two-piece suit and a frilly blouse. No attempt to impress the court with a sombre appearance.

'What can we talk about?' she said as she stirred her coffee.

'What's your favourite piece of music?'

She laughed. 'Either Josephine Baker singing *J'ai deux amours* or the Mendelssohn fiddle concerto.'

'Favourite flower?'

'Daisies in a field. Marguerites.'

'Favourite food?'

'Chocolate eclairs.' She laughed.

'And favourite book?'

'Elizabeth Smart's *By Grand Central Station I sat down and wept.*'

And then Maclean came for them and the grimness of the corridors set her trembling again.

Porter sat listening, watching her face as the questions were put to her. Sir Geoffrey was silky and polite but he was there to do a job. A demolition job.

'You admit that you abused your husband on occasions, using foul language.'

'No, I don't admit anything of the sort.'

Sir Geoffrey raised his ginger eyebrows in surprise as he looked at his notes. 'But you have already agreed that you said: "You lying sod get out of my sight", wouldn't you say that was foul language?'

'I was angry at something he'd done. He'd . . .'

'Thank you, Mrs Pryke. Now let me come to the question of violence.' Sir Geoffrey looked up quickly at her. 'Are you a violent woman, Mrs Pryke? Do you have a violent temper?'

'I can be tormented into being angry if that's what you call violence.'

'Have you ever struck your husband, Mrs Pryke?'

'I slapped his face once. Nothing more than that.'

'Did he ever strike you?'

'No.'

'I see. But when you – as you put it – slapped his face, it was with sufficient force to injure his eye. Yes?'

'It cracked his contact lens. That's all.'

'Causing damage enough to keep him from his office for ten days.'

'That was the time it took to replace the lens. Nothing more.'

'Of course not.' Sir Geoffrey smiled at the jury. 'Just a wifely love tap.' Then Sir Geoffrey's voice was very soft as he looked at her. 'I must ask you one last question Mrs Pryke. I want you to listen very carefully.' Sir Geoffrey glanced at the jury and then back at the witness box. 'Mrs Pryke. Have you ever killed a man?'

Porter saw the blood drain from her face and her knuckles were white as they grasped the edge of the box. Then she said quietly, 'Yes. But that was . . .'

'Mrs Pryke, how many men have you killed in your lifetime?'

She took a deep breath. 'Two, and in both cases . . .'

'Thank you, Mrs Pryke. And one last question to you. In the case of one of the men you killed you used a pistol. What did you use in the other case?'

'I used a knife.'

'You stabbed him several times? Three or four times perhaps.'

'I don't remember.'

'I see.' Sir Geoffrey raised his eyebrows in the general direction of the Press benches. 'That will be all, thank you Mrs Pryke.'

Mathew Porter stood up slowly. 'My Lord, I know we are already running late but after my learned colleague's last few questions I should like a few moments more so that this matter does not hang over the night.'

His Lordship nodded. 'Don't be too long, Mr Porter, but carry on.'

Porter turned to his client. 'Mrs Pryke, would you tell the

17

court who the two men were who you killed.'

'I don't remember their names.'

'Their ranks perhaps. Or the circumstances.'

'One was a Gestapo officer and one was a sergeant in the Sicherheitsdienst. The Nazi Security Service.'

'Tell us very briefly what happened.'

'They had arrested the seven leading people in my SOE network. I killed the two men to set my colleagues free.'

'This was in wartime? In German-occupied France?'

'Yes.'

'And for this you were awarded the Order of the British Empire. You received it from King George the Sixth himself at Buckingham Palace.'

'Yes.'

'And was the plaintiff, your husband, aware of these facts even before he married you?'

'Yes. He accompanied me to the medal presentation.'

'Thank you, Mrs Pryke.' Porter turned to look at the Judge. 'My Lord, tomorrow I should like to suggest to the court that this application is dismissed on the grounds that the evidence put forward to denigrate my client's character has been done with deliberate malice and was to a large part intended to create both a totally false impression of the real facts and an attempt to deceive the court . . .'

'Mr Porter. Can we leave the rest of it until tomorrow at ten?'

'As your Lordship pleases.'

Porter and Maclean had walked over to the Wig and Pen with their client and taken a table at the far end. She seemed to have recovered from her nervousness.

'Thanks for what you said. About the SOE business.'

'I ought not to have needed to say it. It was a scurrilous attack on their part and I'm surprised that Sir Geoffrey would wear it. The rest was pretty thin but to my mind that last bit went too far. I don't think His Lordship liked it too much. What do you think, Jamie?'

18

Maclean grinned. 'I'd say there's a good chance of them throwing it out tomorrow.'

Jill Pryke looked at Maclean. 'Does that mean he might not get a divorce?'

'It's quite possible, my dear, and I'd think you might even be able to consider bringing a cross-petition citing today as your reasons.'

As they chatted Porter was aware of his client's silence and eventually he said, 'What's the problem?'

She took a deep breath. 'I want to withdraw. Let it be undefended.'

'But why?'

'I don't want to be married to him any more.'

'You can cross-petition like I said.'

'That would take time. I'd like to be free of him tomorrow.'

Porter looked at Maclean who said, 'Think about it overnight. Don't rush into it.'

She shook her head as she looked at Porter. 'Don't think I'm not grateful. I am. Terribly grateful. But hearing you sticking up for me in court was enough. I felt hounded, but not anymore. I just want to be free of it. All of it.'

Maclean said, 'If you're sure that's what you want.'

'It is,' she said as she stood up. 'I'd like to leave while I feel happy, if you don't mind.'

She shook hands with Porter, and Maclean walked her into the Strand, waved down a taxi for her and walked back to Porter at the table.

'My God.. Human beings. What a turmoil we're always in.'

Porter smiled. 'She's right you know. She should have gone this way right at the start. She's only doing what we both counselled her to do. But she's had her bite back in court. And why shouldn't she?' He paused and looked at Maclean. 'I didn't realise until this afternoon what her little secret was that you wouldn't let me know.'

'OK. Why this afternoon?'

19

Porter smiled. 'Watching Sir Geoffrey. He was loving every minute of it. Hounding her. Hating her. They're two of a kind aren't they? Him and Pryke. Brothers in sex.'

Maclean nodded. 'He made a declaration when he was called up, about his . . . er . . . predilections. That's why he wasn't in the services. The marriage must have been hopeless from the start.'

'Ah well. All's well that ends well.'

The small boy was looking at the things on the table.

'What's the music, daddy?'

'It's a violin concerto by a chap named Mendelssohn.'

'What a funny name.'

'It isn't really, it's just a foreign name.'

'And you always give her these things as well as a proper present. Why eclairs and a bunch of daisies and always this same book?'

'A long time ago we sat in a rather gloomy tea place and I asked her about her favourite things. These were the things she chose.'

'Were you two married then?'

'No. It was a long time ago.'

'Did you like her when you had tea with her?'

'I admired her. I got to like her later.'

'Why?'

'Oh lots of reasons. I'll tell you some day when I've worked out what they are. She's coming in from the garden now. Thinks we've forgotten her birthday.'

The small boy smiled. 'Women are funny aren't they?'

Simon Brett

DON'T KNOW MUCH ABOUT ART

I have been described as not very bright. Partly, I reckon it's my size. People who look like me have appeared as dumb villains in too many movies and television series. And if you've had a background as a professional wrestler, you find the general public doesn't have too many expectations of you as an intellect.

Also, I have to face it, there have been one or two unfortunate incidents in my past. Jobs that didn't turn out exactly like they was planned. Like when I was in the getaway car outside that bank and I drove off with the wrong passengers. Or when I got muddled after that bullion robbery and delivered it all back to the security firm. Or when I wrote my home address on that ransom demand. OK, silly mistakes, sort of thing anyone could do in the heat of the moment, but I'm afraid it's the kind of thing that sticks in people's minds and I have got a bit of a reputation in the business as a dumbo.

Result of it all is, most of the jobs I get tend to be – to put it mildly – intellectually undemanding. In fact, the approach of most of the geysers who hire me seems to be, 'We couldn't find a blunt instrument, so you'll have to do.'

Now, of course, my own view of my mental capacity doesn't exactly coincide with that, but a chap has to live, and a recession isn't the time you can afford to be choosy. I mean, you read all this about rising crime figures, but you mustn't get the impression from that that villains are doing well. No, we feel the pinch like anyone else. For a start, there's a lot more blokes trying to muscle in. Side-effect of unemployment, of course, and most of them are really amateurs, but they do queer the pitch for us professionals. They undercut our rates and bring into the business a kind of dishonesty that I'm sure wasn't there when I started. The cake isn't that much bigger than it ever was, and there's a hell of a lot more blokes trying to get slices.

Result is, I take anything I'm offered . . . driving, bouncing, frightening, looming (often booked for looming I am, on account of my size). No, I'll do anything. Short of contract killing. Goes against my principles, that and mugging old ladies. As I say, it's no time to be choosy. When this country's got more than three million unemployed, you just got to put off your long-term ambitions, forget temporarily about career structure, and be grateful you got a job of any sort.

So when I was offered the Harbinger Hall job, never crossed my mind to turn it down. Apart from anything else, it sounded easy and the pay was bloody good. Five grand for a bit of petty larceny . . . well, that can't be bad, can it? Sure, there was always the risk of getting nicked, but didn't look like there'd be any rough stuff. Mind you, never be quite sure in stately homes. Tend to be lots of spears and shotguns and that stuck on the walls, so there's always the danger that someone might have a fit of temperament and cop hold of one of those.

Still, five grand for a weekend's work in a slow autumn was good money.

The initial contact come through Wally Clinton, which I must say surprised me. It was Wally I was driving to Heathrow after that jeweller's job the time I run out of petrol, so I didn't think I was exactly his Flavour of the Month. Still, shows how you can misjudge people. Here he was letting bygones be bygones and even putting a nice bit of work my way. Take back all that I said about him at the Black Dog last New Year's Eve.

Anyway, so Wally gets in touch, asks if I'm in the market and when I says yes, tells me to go and meet this bloke, 'Mr Loxton', in this sauna club off St Martin's Lane.

Strange sauna club it was. Not a girl in sight. I think it actually must've been for geysers who wanted to have saunas. All neat and tidy, no little massage cubicles with plastic curtains, no funny smell, no nasty bits of screwed-up tissue on the floor. Most peculiar.

Bloke on the door was expecting me. Give me a big white towel and showed me into a changing-room that was all very swish with pine and clean tiles. He told me to take my clothes off, put on the towel and go into the sauna. Mr Loxton would join me shortly.

Don't mind telling you, I felt a bit of a grapefruit sitting on this wooden shelf with nothing on but this towel. When I first went in I sat on the top shelf, but blimey it was hot. Soon realised it got cooler the lower you went, so I went to the bottom one. Still uncomfortably hot, mind. Geyser my size really sweats when he sweats.

I tried to work out why Mr Loxton had chosen this place for the meet. I mean, a sauna's good if you're worried the opposition might've got shooters. Isn't anywhere you can put one when you've got your clothes off. Nowhere comfortable, anyway. But this wasn't that kind of encounter.

On the other hand, it wasn't bad if you didn't want to be identified. The lights in the sauna was low and it was a bit steamy. Also, people don't look the same when they're starkers. Oh, I know they do lots of corpse identification from secret birthmarks and moles on the body and that, but the average bloke without clothes on doesn't look like himself. For a start, next time you see him, chances are he'll be dressed, and you'd be surprised how many clues you get to what a person's like from what they wear. I reckoned Mr Loxton was meeting there to maintain the old incog.

I felt even more sure of that when he come in. He had a big towel round him under his armpits like me, but he also got a small one draped over his head like a boxer. He didn't turn his face towards me, but immediately went over to a wooden bucket in the corner, picked out a ladleful of water and poured it over this pile of stones. Well, that really got the steam going, and when he did turn towards me, he wasn't no more than a blur.

'You are Billy Gorse.'

I admitted it. Wasn't spoken like a question, anyway, more a statement.

'Thank you for coming. Wally Clinton recommended you for a job that needs doing.'

He might have hid his face with all the towels and the steam, but he had a voice that was really distinctive. Private school, you know, and a bit prissy. I'm good with voices. Knew I'd recognise his if I ever heard it again.

I stayed stumm, waiting for the details, and he went on. 'What I want you to do, Gorse, is to steal a painting.'

'Blimey,' I said, 'I don't know much about art.'

'You don't need to.'

'But surely . . . paintings . . . I mean specialist work, isn't it? Not like walking in and nicking someone's video. If a painting's any good, it's got security systems all round it. And then finding a fence who'll handle them sort of goods—'

'All that side is taken care of. All I said I wanted you to do was to steal a painting.'

'You mean I'd be, like, part of a gang?'

'There's no need for you to know anything about anyone else involved. All you have to do is to follow instructions witho need for you to know anything about anyone else involved. All you have to do is to follow instructions without question.'

'I can do that.'

'Good. Wally said you could. You do the job on the last weekend of October.'

'Where?'

'Have you heard of Harbinger Hall?'

I shook my head.

'Then I suppose you haven't heard of the Harbinger Madonna either.'

'Who's she?'

'"She" is the painting you are going to steal.'

'Oh. Well, like I said, I don't know much about art.'

'No.' His voice sounded sort of pleased about that. Smug.

He asked me where he could send my instructions. I nearly give him my home address, but something told me hold my horses, so I give him the name of Red Rita's gaff. She often holds mail for me, on account of services rendered what I needn't go into here.

Then Mr Loxton reached into his towel and pulled out a polythene bag. Thought of everything, he did. Didn't want the notes to get damp.

'Five hundred in there. Two thousand when you get your instructions. Second half on completion of the job.' He rose through the steam. 'Stay here another ten minutes. If you appear in the changing room before I've left the building, the contract's cancelled.' He reached for the door handle.

'Oh, Mr Loxton . . .'

His reaction was that half-second slow, which confirmed that he wasn't using his real name. No great surprise. Very few of the geysers I deal with do. Not for me, that. Always stick to 'Billy Gorse'. Only time I tried anything different, I forgot who I was half-way through the job.

'What did you want, Mr Gorse?'

I'd got what I wanted, but I said, 'Oh, just to say thank you for the job, Mr Loxton.'

He done a sort of snort and walked out the sauna.

Long ten minutes it was in that heat. When I come out I was sweating like a Greek cheese.

Instructions come the following week as per. I went down Red Rita's for reasons that aren't any of your business and after a bit, she give me this thick brown envelope. Just my name on it. No stamps, nothing like that. Just come through her letter-box. She didn't see who dropped it.

I didn't open it till I got back to my place next morning. First I counted the money. Fifties, forty of them all present and correct. Then there was this postcard of some bird in blue with this nipper on her knee. That was presumably the picture I was going to nick. I didn't take much notice of it, but unfolded the typewritten sheet of instructions.

No mention of my name and they wasn't signed either. Plain paper, no other clues to where it might've come from. It was all typed in capital letters, which I must say got my goat a bit. Reckon Wally Clinton'd been casting aspersions on my literacy, the cheeky devil. Anyway, what I had to do was spelled out very clear.

FIRST – FILL IN THE ENCLOSED BOOKING FORM, BOOKING YOURSELF INTO THE 'STATELY HOME WEEKEND' AT HARBINGER HALL FOR THE 29TH AND 30TH OCTOBER. SEND THE FULL PAYMENT BY MONEY ORDER. (ALL YOUR EXPENSES WILL BE REPAID.)

SECOND – THIS FRIDAY, 21ST OCTOBER, TRAVEL DOWN TO HARBINGER HALL AND TAKE THE CONDUCTED TOUR OF THE BUILDING (THESE RUN EVERY HOUR ON THE HOUR BETWEEN 10 A.M. AND 4 P.M.). WHEN YOU REACH THE GREAT HALL, LOOK CAREFULLY AT THE PAINTING OF THE MADONNA, NOTING THE VISIBLE SECURITY ARRANGEMENTS AROUND IT.

WHEN THE TOUR REACHES THE END OF THE LONG GALLERY UPSTAIRS, LINGER BEHIND THE GROUP. AS THE REST OF THEM GO INTO THE BLUE BEDROOM, OPEN THE DOOR LABELLED 'PRIVATE' AT THE END OF THE GALLERY. YOU WILL FIND YOURSELF AT

THE TOP OF A SMALL STAIRCASE. GO DOWN THIS QUICKLY AND YOU WILL FIND YOURSELF IN A SMALL LOBBY. ON THE WALL OPPOSITE THE FOOT OF THE STAIRS YOU WILL SEE THE BOXES CONTROLLING THE BUILDING'S ALARM SYSTEM. THESE ARE OPERATED BY A KEY, BUT YOU WILL SEE THE WIRES WHICH COME OUT OF THE TOP OF THE BOXES. WHEN YOU ACTUALLY COME TO STEAL THE MADONNA, YOU WILL CUT THROUGH THESE WIRES. HAVING SEEN THEIR POSITION, RETURN AS QUICKLY AS POSSIBLE UP THE STAIRS AND REJOIN YOUR GROUP. COMPLETE THE REST OF THE TOUR AND RETURN HOME WITHOUT FURTHER INVESTIGATION.

FURTHER INSTRUCTIONS WILL FOLLOW NEXT WEEK. MEMORISE THE DETAILS IN THESE SHEETS AND THEN BURN THEM.

I done like I was told and before the Friday I got a confirmation of my booking on this 'Stately Home Weekend'. I read the brochure on that and I must say it didn't really sound my scene. Tours of the grounds, lectures on the history of the place, full mediaeval banquet on the Saturday night, farewell tea with Lord Harbinger on the Sunday. I mean, my idea of a fun weekend is going down Southend with a few mates and putting back a few beers. Still, I'd put up with a lot for five grand.

So, the Friday I do as I'm told. Get the train out to Limmerton, and from there they've got this courtesy bus takes you out to Harbinger Hall.

Not a bad little gaff old Lord Harbinger's got, I'll say that for him. Don't know any more about architecture than I do about art, but I can tell it's old. Don't build places like that nowadays, not with blooming great pillars in front of the door and all them windows and twiddly bits on the roof.

Nice position and all. It's high, like on top of this hill, looking out over all the rest of the countryside. That's how you first see it in the bus from the station. As you get nearer, you lose sight for a bit, because it's a really steep hill with trees. So you sort of zigzag up this drive, which is really a bit hairy and makes you glad the old bus's got decent brakes. And then suddenly you come out the top and you're right in front of the house and it's blooming big. And there's car parks off to the right and left, but the bus drops you pretty well by the front door.

I looked around as I got out. You know, some of these stately homes've got sort of zoos and funfairs and that, you know, a bit of entertainment. And, since I had to spend a whole weekend there, I thought it'd be nice to know there'd be something interesting to do. But no such luck. Place hadn't been developed like that. Maybe the grounds wasn't big enough.

In fact, not only hadn't the place been developed, it looked a bit tatty. I mean that sort of gaff isn't my style. Blimey, if I owned it, I'd knock it down and put up a nice executive Regency-style townhouse with double garage and Italian suite bathroom. But even I could tell this one needed a few grand spending on it.

And if my busload was anything to go by, the few grand wasn't going to come very quickly from tourists. OK, end of the season and that, but there wasn't many of us. Had to wait around till a few more come from the car parks before they'd start our guided tour, and then it was only about a dozen of us. Well, at a couple of sovs a head, takes you a long time to make money that way.

The guide what took us round had done the trip a few thousand times and obviously hadn't enjoyed it much even the first time. The spiel come out like a recording, jokes and all. Didn't look a happy man.

And what he said was dead boring. I never got on with history at school, couldn't see the percentage in it, so all his cobblers about what Duke built which bit and when didn't do a lot for me. And to think that I'd got a whole weekend of lectures on it coming up. I began to think I was going to earn my five grand.

Anyway, eventually we get to the Great Hall, and I see this picture all the fuss is about. Didn't go on it much in the postcard; the real thing's just the same, only bigger. Not big, though, compared to some of the numbers they got on the walls. I don't know, two foot by eighteen inches maybe. Don't know why they wanted to nick this one. Some of them was ten times the size, must've been worth a lot more. Still, not my decision. And a good thing, come to think of it, that they didn't want me to walk out with one of the twenty foot numbers under my arm.

So the picture's just this Mum and her sprog. Frame was nice, mind. All gold and wiggly, like my brother-in-law's got round the cocktail bar in his lounge. And at the bottom of the frame there's this little brass plate nailed on. It says:

MADONNA AND CHILD
Giacomo Palladino
Florentine
(1473–1539)

Never heard of the git myself.

Anyway, I'd memorised my instructions like a good boy, so I have a good butchers at the pic. Can't see a lot in the way of security. I mean, there's a sort of purple rope strung between uprights to keep the punters six feet away from the wall, but that isn't going to stop anyone. Of course, there might be some photo-electric beam or some rocker device what sounds the alarm if you actually touch the thing. I step over the rope to take a closer look.

'Art-lover, are we, sir?' asks this sarcastic voice behind me.

I turn round and see this bloke in uniform. Not the guide, he's up the other end blathering about some king or other. No, this geyser's just some sort of security guard I noticed hanging around when we arrived.

'No,' I says, with what people have described as my winning

smile. 'Don't know a blind thing about art.'

'Then why are you studying the Madonna so closely?'

I'm about to say that I'm just interested in what security arrangements she got, and then I twig that this might not be so clever, so I do this big shrug and step back over the rope and join up with the other punters. I glance back as we're leaving the hall and this guard's giving me a really beady look.

Upstairs I follow the instructions without sweat. Dawdle doing the old untied shoe-lace routine while the rest troop in to hear the history of the Blue Bedroom, quick look round to see I'm on my own in the gallery, then through the old 'Private' door and down the stairs.

It's just like they said it would be. These big metal-covered boxes opposite me with coloured lights and chrome keyholes on them. And at the top the wires. Not that thick. Quick snip with the old metal-cutters. No prob.

I think for a minute. I know some of these systems got a sort of fail-safe so's they sound off if anyone tampers with the wiring. For a moment I wonder if someone's trying to set me up. Certainly are one or two geysers what I have sort of inadvertently offended in the course of my varied career, but this'd be a bloody elaborate way of getting their own back. Anyway, there's the two and a half grand I already got. Nobody's going to spend that kind of bread just to fix me. I hurry back upstairs again.

I've just closed the door when I see the security guard coming in the other end of the Long Gallery. Don't know whether he saw me or not, but he still looks beady. 'Looking for something, sir?' he calls out, sarcastic again.

'Little boys' room,' I say, and nip along to the Blue Bedroom.

Next package arrives the Wednesday, three days before I'm due on my Stately Home Weekend. I'm actually round at Red Rita's when we hear it plop through the letter-box, but needless to say by the time I open the front door to see who brought it, there's nobody in sight.

Since the whole thing's getting a bit close and Red Rita's tied up with someone else, I open the package there. There's money in it, which I wasn't expecting this time. It's in fives and ones and a bit of change and covers my expenses so far. What I paid to book the weekend, return fare London to Limmerton, even the two quid for my guided tour. Someone's done their research. Makes me feel good. Nice to know you're dealing with geysers who knows what's what. There's a lot of berks in this business.

As well as the money there's a car key. Just one, on a little ring attached to a plain yellow plastic tag. And of course there's the instructions. Block capitals again, which miffs me a bit. Again, they're so clear an idiot could understand them. I wonder if someone's trying to tell me something.

> ON THE MORNING OF SATURDAY, 29TH OCTOBER AT 9 A.M., GO TO THE UNDERGROUND CAR PARK IN CAVENDISH SQUARE. THERE, IN BAY NUMBER 86, YOU WILL FIND A RED PEUGEOT WHICH YOU CAN OPEN AND START WITH THE ENCLOSED KEY. ON THE BACK SEAT WILL BE A LARGE SUITCASE, TO WHICH YOU WILL TRANSFER YOUR CLOTHES, ETC. FOR THE WEEKEND. *DO NOT REMOVE ANYTHING FROM THE SUIT-CASE*.
>
> IN THE GLOVE COMPARTMENT OF THE CAR YOU WILL FIND MONEY TO PAY THE PARKING CHARGE. DRIVE DIRECTLY TO HARBINGER HALL. GIVEN NORMAL TRAFFIC CONDITIONS, YOU SHOULD ARRIVE THERE AT ABOUT HALF-PAST TWELVE, JUST IN TIME FOR THE BUFFET LUNCH WHICH OPENS THE STATELY HOME WEEKEND.
>
> DURING THE WEEKEND TAKE PART IN ALL

THE ACTIVITIES OFFERED AND GENERALLY BEHAVE AS NATURALLY AS POSSIBLE. ABOVE ALL, DO NOT DRAW ATTENTION TO YOURSELF.

THE MOMENT FOR THE THEFT OF THE MADONNA WILL COME LATE ON THE SUNDAY AFTERNOON WHEN THE TOUR GUESTS ARE ABOUT TO LEAVE. AT THE END OF THESE OCCASIONS THE TRADITION HAS DEVELOPED OF LORD HARBINGER, HIS FAMILY AND STAFF LINING UP IN THE FRONT HALL TO SAY GOODBYE TO THEIR GUESTS. THE PREMISES WILL BE CLEARED OF DAY VISITORS BY FOUR O'CLOCK ON THIS, THE LAST DAY OF THE SEASON. THERE WILL BE NO STAFF GUARDING THE MADONNA.

FOLLOW THESE INSTRUCTIONS EXACTLY. AFTER TEA WITH LORD HARBINGER, THE STATELY HOME WEEKEND GUESTS ARE GIVEN HALF AN HOUR TO PACK AND ASKED TO APPEAR IN THE FRONT HALL AT SIX TO SAY THEIR GOODBYES AND GET THE COACH TO THE STATION OR GO TO THEIR OWN CARS. DO ANY PACKING YOU HAVE TO AND GO DOWN TO THE FRONT HALL AT TEN TO SIX, *LEAVING YOUR SUITCASE IN YOUR BEDROOM*. WHEN MOST OF THE OTHER GUESTS ARE DOWNSTAIRS, MAKE A SHOW OF REMEMBERING YOUR SUITCASE AND HURRY BACK TO YOUR BEDROOM TO GET IT. *THE NEXT BIT HAS TO BE DONE QUICKLY*. GO FROM THE PRIVATE APARTMENTS TO THE LONG GALLERY AND DOWN THE STAIRCASE TO THE ALARM BOXES. CUT THROUGH THE WIRES AT THE TOP OF THE BOXES. THERE IS A DOOR TO THE RIGHT OF THESE WHICH LEADS

34

DIRECTLY INTO THE GREAT HALL. GO
THROUGH, GO STRAIGHT TO THE MADONNA
AND REPLACE THE ORIGINAL PAINTING WITH
THE COPY IN YOUR SUITCASE. IT WILL JUST BE
A MATTER OF UNHOOKING THE PICTURE AT
THE BACK. WITH THE ALARMS NEUTRALISED,
THERE ARE NO OTHER RESTRAINING
DEVICES.

PUT THE ORIGINAL PAINTING IN YOUR
SUITCASE AND RETURN UPSTAIRS THE WAY
YOU CAME. GO BACK TO YOUR ROOM AND
THEN GO DOWN THE MAIN STAIRCASE TO THE
FRONT HALL. THE WHOLE OPERATION
SHOULD TAKE YOU LESS THAN FIVE MINUTES
AND WILL NOT BE NOTICED IN THE
CONFUSION OF THE GUESTS' GOODBYES. JOIN
IN WITH THESE AND BEHAVE PERFECTLY
NATURALLY. ALLOW ONE OF THE STAFF TO
TAKE YOUR SUITCASE OUT TO YOUR CAR, AND
ASK HIM TO PUT IT ON THE BACK SEAT.

DRIVE STRAIGHT BACK TO LONDON.
RETURN THE CAR TO THE CAVENDISH SQUARE
GARAGE, PARKING IT IN BAY 86 OR AS NEAR TO
THAT AS YOU CAN GET. REMOVE YOUR OWN
BELONGINGS FROM THE SUITCASE, BUT
LEAVE THE CASE ITSELF AND THE PAINTING,
ALONG WITH THE CAR KEY AND PARKING
TICKET INSIDE. THEN LOCK THE CAR BY
PRESSING DOWN THE LOCKING BUTTON
INSIDE AND CLOSING THE DOOR WITH THE
HANDLE HELD OUT.

WHEN YOU RETURN TO THE ADDRESS USED
BEFORE, YOU WILL FIND THE SECOND
TWO AND A HALF THOUSAND POUNDS
WAITING FOR YOU.

AS BEFORE, MEMORISE THESE INSTRUC-
TIONS *AND BURN THEM*.

Now I got my principles, but crime is my business and it's a
sort of natural reaction for me to have a look at any plan what
comes up and see if there's anything in it for me. You know,
anything extra, over and above the basic fee.

And, having read my instructions, I couldn't help noticing
that, assuming all went well with the actual nicking, from the
moment I left Harbinger Hall on the Sunday night I was going
to be in temporary possession of an extremely valuable
painting.

Now I been in my line of work long enough to know that
nasty things can happen to villains carrying off the goods. You
hear cases of them being hi-jacked by other gangs, mugged,
somehow getting lost on the way to their hand-over, all that.
And though I didn't fancy any of those happening to me, I
wasn't so down on the idea of them *appearing* to happen to me. I
mean, if I'm found on the roadside with the side of my motor
bashed in, a bump on my head and the suitcase gone, the bosses
won't be able to *prove* I knew the bloke who done it.

Don't get me wrong. I wasn't planning anything particular,
just sort of going through the possibilities in my mind. Like I
said, I don't know anything about art, but I do know that you
need extremely specialised help if you're trying to unload a
well-known stolen painting.

One of the advantages of Red Rita's line of work is that she
does get to meet a big variety of people and when I mentioned,
casual like, that I wanted a bit of background on the art scene, it
turned out she did just happen to know this geyser who was a
dealer in the less public transactions of international
art-collectors. And he was another of the many who owed her a
favour and yes, she'd be quite happy to fix up a meet. For me,
darling, anything.

I suppose I shouldn't have been surprised, if I'd thought about it. I mean, bent bookies are still bookies, bent solicitors do their stuff in solicitors' offices, but I really hadn't expected a bent art dealer to work out of a posh little gallery off Bond Street. Still, that was the address Red Rita give me, and when I got there it seemed that Mr Depaldo was expecting me. The sniffy tart at the desk said she would just check he was free and left me looking at a series of pics of what seemed to be a nasty accident in the kitchens of a Chinese restaurant. I don't know how people buy that stuff. I mean, if you can't tell what it's meant to be, how do you know you're not being taken for a ride? Don't get me wrong, I'm not against all art. My brother-in-law's got this collection of sunsets painted on black velvet and with those, well, you can *see* they're good. But a lot of this modern stuff . . . forget it.

So I'm shown up to Mr Depaldo's poncy little office, and he's a real smoothie. Striped shirt, bow tie, you know the number. If I didn't know about his connection with Red Rita, I'd have put him down as a wooftah.

But her hold is clearly strong. Plain from the start he don't want to see me, but Rita's threatened to blow the lid on something if he won't. So he just about managed to be polite.

I ask him if it's possible to sell a stolen picture and he says, through a lot of unnecessary grammar, that it is.

Then I mention the Harbinger Madonna, and he sort of perks up like a conman spotting a mark. And I ask him how much he reckons it's worth.

'Well, it's hard to tell. Prices at auction are so unpredictable. I mean, there aren't many Palladinos around, certainly no others of that quality. The last one to come on the market was a Saint Sebastian back in '68. Went to eight hundred.'

Didn't seem that much to me. I mean, paying me five grand and only getting eight hundred for the goods, well, that's no way to run a whelk-stall.

Old Depaldo must've twigged what I was thinking, because he says, rather vinegary, 'Eight hundred *thousand*, of course. But that was fifteen years ago. And an inferior work. If the Madonna came to auction now, she must go to at least two.'

'Two?' I queried, not wanting to be caught out again.

'Million.'

'That's at auction?'

'Yes. Of course, a . . . private deal wouldn't realise nearly as much.'

'Like what?'

You know, all fences give you the same pause before they come up with a figure. Doesn't matter if you're talking a colour telly, a lorryload of booze or a *Last Supper*, they all hesitate before they cheat you. 'Maybe one. Say seven hundred and fifty to be safe.'

Even if he'd been telling the truth, it sounded like a lot of money. Made my five grand for actually taking the risk and doing the job look a bit pathetic.

'And if it did . . . become available, you could handle it?'

He nodded, looking sort of eager. Obviously he knew there was a lot more in it for him than he let on. 'There are only two people in London who could make the arrangements, and I'm one of them.'

'But I'm the first one who's talked to you about it?'

'Yes.'

So perhaps my bosses had got a deal set up with the other geyser. 'What's your commission rate, by the way?'

'Sixty per cent,' he says, cool as an ice-cream down the neck. 'You see, in these matters the risk must be judged in relation to how much one has to lose.'

Meaning he'd got his poncy gallery and his sniffy tart downstairs and his international reputation; and I was just a cheap heavy. I let it pass. Reckoned I could work out some fine tuning on the figures later if it became necessary.

'Any idea,' he asks, really keen now, 'when this exceptional property might come on the market?'

'No,' I tell him. 'Only asking for information, aren't I?'

He looks a bit miffed.

'But if it ever was to come up,' I go on, 'you'd be interested in handling it?'

'Oh yes,' he says.

I haven't made any plans yet, mind. But it is nice to have things sorted out in case you need them.

Saturday morning I do like a good boy should. Get to Cavendish Square car park on the nose of nine, find the car in Bay 86. Red Peugeot, like they said. Ordinary saloon, not one of the hatchback jobs. The key opens the door and fits the ignition. I try it on the boot, which seems to be locked, but it doesn't fit. Needs a different key. Never mind.

On the back seat there's this suitcase as per. One of those that sort of opens up like a big wallet with a zip three-quarters of the way round. Then inside there's straps to hold your clothes in. One side, strapped in, is this hard rectangular package wrapped in cloth. Got to be the copy of the painting, but I don't think it's the moment to have a dekko. I take my gear out of the polythene carrier I got it in and strap the lot in the other side. Just clothes, shaving tackle. And a pair of metal-cutters. Oh, and a thing called a priest. Little stick with a weighted tip. Fishermen use them to finish off fish. Mine's clobbered a few slimy customers in its time, and all. Wouldn't ever carry a shooter, but the priest's handy.

Car starts first turn of the key, so I reckon it had only been left there that morning. In the glove compartment there's the parking ticket. Clocked in 8:12. Pity I hadn't thought to arrive earlier. Be nice to know who I was dealing with, apart from the steamy 'Mr Loxton'.

There was the right money in the glove compartment for the parking. Seemed a bit steep for such a short stay, and I mentioned this to the bloke at the barrier.

'Rates just gone up, mate. Here's the new tariff.' And he give me a printed sheet with my receipt.

I shoved it in my pocket. I should worry. Wasn't my money I was spending.

*   *   *

I never really thought it would be, but the Stately Home Weekend was way off my scene. I mean, we was treated all right, you know, all the staff deferential and that, trying to give you the feeling of being privileged, but you got the feeling they didn't really mean it, like they was sniggering behind your back all the time.

OK, some things we was allowed to do that the ordinary day-trippers wasn't. We could leave our cars directly in front of the house, we could go through most of the doors marked 'Private', we was actually allowed to *sit* on the chairs. But all the time they was pretending to treat us like regular house party guests, the staff seemed to be just watching out for us to make fools of ourselves. I mean, like turning up in the wrong clothes or not picking the right knives and forks at meals, they really seemed to be on the lookout for that sort of thing. And I'm afraid for me it was particularly difficult. Social graces didn't figure large in the Borstal educational curriculum.

Mind you, the other punters seemed to lap it up. I saw they was getting the old sneers from the staff just as much as I was, but they didn't seem to notice. They really thought they was being treated just like house-guests, like they was there by personal invite of Lord Harbinger and not paying through the nose for the privilege of lounging around his gaff and seeing him for a rationed hour and a half of tea and farewells on the Sunday afternoon.

Also, let's face it, they wasn't really my sort of people. I daresay I got a lot of flaws in my character, but one thing nobody's ever called me is a snob. And that's what this lot was, every one of them.

A lot of them was Americans and in fact they was generally less offensive than the English ones. I mean, their grasp on culture was so sketchy that all they seemed to do was keep saying how old everything was. Apparently Harbinger Hall had been featured in some naff television series that they'd seen over there and they spent a lot of time walking round the place acting out their favourite bits and taking photos of each other in various settings. Funny lot, the Yanks, I always thought that.

Still, they was at least friendly. The English punters reckoned as soon as they saw me that I wasn't 'their sort of person'. Dead right they was too. I wouldn't want to be some nasty little factory owner who, just because he's made a bit of bread, reckons he can go around buying breeding. I may not have a lot in the way of social gloss, but at least it's all mine.

Anyway, the English ones certainly disapproved of me. I'd catch them talking behind their hands about me when I come in the room. 'Sticks out like a sore thumb,' I heard one cheeky little pickle-manufacturer say. 'You'd think they'd vet the applications of people who come on these weekends.'

Under other circumstances I'd have pushed the little git's false teeth out the other end, but I remembered that I wasn't meant to be drawing attention to myself so I laid off him.

You'll have got the impression by now that the company wasn't that great, and let me tell you the entertainment, so-called, was even worse. Dear oh dear. I already told you my views on history, and I really thought that old git of a guide had said everything there was to say and a bit more about Harbinger Hall when I done my day-trip. Don't you believe it. For the Stately Home Weekend they got in blooming Professors of History to take us through the lot, Duke by Duke. Then another berk come and took us through the family portraits and, as if that weren't enough, some bloody snooty old blue-rinse give us a lecture on eighteenth century house-keeping. Tell you, I done some boring jobs in my time, but I'd rather spend a solid week watching for some fence to come out of his front door than ever sit through that lot again.

The Mediaeval Banquet wasn't no better. My idea of a good Saturday night is going out for a few beers and, if you're feeling a bit exotic, ending up at the Chinkie or the Indian; not sitting in front of seventeen knives and forks while gits march up and down holding up stuffed pigs and peacocks. As a general rule, I don't mind music, either – good sing-song round the Joanna or

41

a nice tape of James Last, Abba, that sort of number; but please God may I never again be put in a position where I have to act natural while listening to a bunch of birds singing madrigals to a lute.

But I stuck at it, like a right little swot. Fixed my mind steadily on the five grand. Or maybe on a bit more than that.

Being the size I am, I got a pretty well-developed appetite, and all them lectures and that had sharpened it a bit, so, even though they wasn't serving anything I fancied, I had a good go at all this stuffed pig and peacock and fruit tarts and what-have-you. Even forced myself to drink some of the mead, which is not an experience I'd recommend to anyone with taste-buds.

Anyway, result of all this is, I wake up in bed round one in the morning with this dreadful heartburn. Well, it's more than heartburn, really. It's that round the chest, but it seems to be moving down the body and turning into something less tasteful. Not to put too fine a point on it, I have to get to the bog in a hurry.

Well, they're real mean with the wattage on the landings and, sense of direction never having been my special subject, I go through all kinds of corridors and staircases before I find what I'm looking for.

And, dear oh dear, when I get there, what a spectacle it is. Blooming great dark wood seat like something out of an old rowing boat, and the pan's got all these pink and blue roses all over it. Out the back there's this sort of plunger like it was going to detonate a bomb. You'd really think in a place like Harbinger Hall they'd get decent facilities. I mean, more like the sort of thing my brother-in-law's got – low-level avocado with matching sink and gold-plated dolphin flush-handle.

Still, I'm in no condition to bother about Lord Harbinger's lack of design sense. It's lock the door, down with the pyjama trousers and settle in for a long session.

Embarrassing though it is to confess, I'm afraid I must've

dozed off. Mead must've got to me. Because next thing I know I'm hearing voices. I don't mean 'hearing voices' like loonies hear; I mean there's a couple of geysers nattering outside the bog door. So I holds my breath (amongst other things) and listens.

Well, first thing is, I recognise one of the voices. Told you I was good on them, didn't I? Yes, you guessed. Mr Loxton from the sauna, wasn't it?

'I saw our contact this afternoon,' he's saying. 'All set up for tomorrow evening. It'll be a quick handover.'

'That's not what I'm worried about. It's the bit before.'

'It'll be fine. I've talked to the staff and it sounds as if the other guests are certainly going to remember him.'

'But if he's as dumb as he appears, are you sure he's capable of actually doing what he's meant to?'

'It's not difficult. If he does blow it, we just call the police and have him arrested.'

'Not keen on that,' the other says sharply. His voice was older, real upper-crusty, sounded like a Cabinet Minister being interviewed, know what I mean. 'Police might want to investigate a bit too deeply. No, we've got to hope the whole affair goes through as planned.'

'I'm sure it will.' Mr Loxton sounds all soothing and . . . what's the word? You know, like a head waiter who thinks he's going to get a big tip.

'Yes. And you're sure he's not suspicious?'

'No chance. Picked with great care. He's as thick as two short planks.'

'Good. Goodnight.'

The older voice was moving away. I unlocked the door dead quiet and risked a quick flash through the crack. One who's just spoken's out of sight, but I see the other just as he's said 'Goodnight.' Mr Loxton's voice. Mean-looking bastard he is when you blow the steam away. But important thing is, he's wearing the striped trousers and that of one of the Harbinger Hall staff. As I suspected, I am part of an inside job.

43

That's not all I've learnt, though. Maybe it's the reference to 'two short planks', which I've heard more than once in my passage through life, but I feel sure Loxton and his chum was talking about me.

I've forgotten my gutrot by the time I get back into bed. Can't be distracted by things like that – need all my mind for thinking.

I can't work out what's happening yet, but I know it's something I don't like. I been set up a few times in my career, and there's a feeling you get when it happens. You don't know the details, but you know something's not kosher. Like when your bird's having it off with someone else.

I go through the whole thing to myself, listening out for the bits that don't ring true. I try to remember if there was any little bits struck me as odd at the time. And I come up with a few.

First, there's the fact that Wally Clinton put up my name. Now, like I explained, he had no reason to sugar-daddy on me. I nearly shopped him once and he had to give a very big birthday present to the boys in blue to get off the hook. Wasn't my fault, but Wally was never bothered by details like that.

My first thought is Wally is just out to get his own back, get me nicked when I cut through the alarm cables, but somehow that don't match the wallpaper. It's too complicated. He don't need to bring in Loxton and all this set-up. And two and a half grand's a month's takings to a smalltimer like Clinton. He's not going to throw it away on me.

'Picked with great care,' Loxton said. What's that mean? I begin to wonder. Think about my reputation in the business, where, as I happened to mention, I am reckoned a complete dumbo who'll do whatever he's told without question.

That's it, of course. Loxton wanted someone guaranteed thick as a bunch of duvets; and Wally Clinton recommended me.

Hurtful though this conclusion is, I don't dwell on it. If that is the case, other things follow. Yes, I am being set up, but set up for something bigger than revenge for Wally. I try to think what else in the deal needs a deodorant.

I remember that right from the start I'd been impressed by the efficiency of the villains I was dealing with. Attention to detail. They'd given me instructions you couldn't go wrong with. They'd paid back my exact expenses. They'd even left the right money for the parking in Cavendish Square.

That thought stopped me. Cavendish Square Garage was where the car was meant to go back to. I was to drive there from Harbinger Hall. On my little lonesome. They'd set the whole thing up real tight until I left the Hall and then I could do what I liked. I know they thought I was thick, but surely even someone thick was going to realise that there was other things they could do with a couple of millionsworth of canvas than leave it in a garage. Considering the care they'd taken with everything else, they really hadn't thought that bit through. Why?

Something else suddenly barged into my mind. I went across to where my bomber jacket was hanging and felt in the pocket. The new price-list the bloke at the garage had given me.

There it was. Give me a nasty turn when I saw it.

The Garage is closed all day Sunday.

They hadn't bothered to think through the details of the hand-over once I'd stolen the painting, because they knew I wasn't going to get that far.

Then I remembered the other thing that didn't fit in. The locked boot of the Peugeot.

Picking locks isn't my Number One talent, but I got a decent set of skeletons and I get by. Could've done the Peugeot boot quicker with a jemmy, but I didn't want no one to see I been snooping. So I was patient and after about ten minutes had it open.

And what a treasure trove my little pencil torch lit up inside. Complete Do-It-Yourself burglar kit. Sets of chisels, jemmies, wire-snips, pliers, big crowbar, the lot. Stethoscope, too, presumably for the old listening-to-the tumblers routine when opening safes. Not that many villains do that nowadays.

Don't use dynamite much either. Not in sticks. Plastic explosive's much easier to handle. Less likely to have accidents. Still, whoever had stocked out that car boot reckoned I might need dynamite for the odd safe-job.

They also reckoned I was going to need something else. The rectangular outline of the suitcase was familiar, and that of the cloth-wrapped object inside even more so. I felt the knobbly ridges of the frame as I undid it.

It was a painting, of course. Same size as the Madonna. Old, like the Madonna. But it wasn't the Madonna. Difficult to see what it was, actually. Or what it had been. The paint was all flaked and stained. Could have been anything. Can't imagine anyone would have given two quid for that one, let alone two million.

But the odd thing about it was that screwed to the frame at the bottom there was this brass plate, which said.

MADONNA AND CHILD
Giacomo Palladino
Florentine
(1473–1539)

Someone was certainly setting me up, but I couldn't right then work out what for.

The Sunday was as boring as the Saturday. Some gamekeeper git give us a long lecture on grouse-shooting; there was a berk who went on about coats of arms; and the 'Traditional Sunday Lunch' was full of gristle. And whoever done the gravy ought to be copped under the Trades Descriptions Act. I mean, if the upper classes have been fed gravy like that since the Norman Conquest, no wonder they're a load of wimps.

The afternoon was, in the words of the old brochure, 'less structured'. That meant, thank God, they couldn't think of anything else to bore us silly with. Guests were encouraged to wander round the grounds until the great moment of tea with Lord Harbinger.

I didn't bother to go out. I just lay on my bed and thought. I was piecing things together. Though nasty things have been said about it, there is nothing wrong with my intellect. It just works slowly. Give it time and it'll get there.

Trouble is, thinking takes it out of me, and I must've dozed off. When I come to, it was quarter to five and the old Royal Command tea had started at four-thirty. I got up in a hurry. Half of me was working out what was up, but the other half was still following instructions. I had to behave naturally, go through the weekend without drawing attention to myself.

As I hurried across the landing, I looked out through the big front window. I could see the red Peugeot parked right outside.

And I could see Mr Loxton closing the boot and moving away from it. Thought I'd be safely inside having my tea, didn't you, Mr Loxton?

The tea give me the last important fact. As soon as I was introduced to Lord Harbinger, it all come together.

'Good afternoon,' he said with a reasonable stab at enthusiasm. 'Delighted to welcome you to Harbinger Hall.'

It was the voice, wasn't it? The bloke Loxton had been speaking to the night before. I realised just how inside an inside job it was.

And I realised other things that give me a nasty trickly feeling in my belly.

Half-past five the tea broke up. Lord Harbinger switched off like a lightbulb and, in spite of the Americans who would have liked to go on mingling with the aristocracy forever, everyone was hustled out of the drawing-room to go and get packed. I went up to my bedroom like the rest.

Wasn't a lot to pack, was there? But for the first time I took a butcher's at the package in my suitcase. After what I seen in the car-boot the night before, could have been anything.

But no. It was a copy of the Madonna. Bloody good, too. I couldn't have told it apart from the real thing. But then I don't know much about art, do I?

Ten to six, following my instructions to the letter, down I go to the hall, leaving my suitcase in the bedroom. There's already a few of the punters milling around and piles of cases. Casual like, I take a glance at these and see, as I expected, that there's one there just like the one I left in the bedroom. Expensive for them on suitcases, this job. Mind you, if it all worked, they'd be able to afford it.

I hear Loxton's voice suddenly, whispering to Lord Harbinger. 'I'll get away as quickly as I can afterwards.'

'Fine,' says the noble peer.

Just before six, most of the punters have arrived and the Harbinger Hall staff are all starting to make a farewell line like something out of a television serial. The Americans think this is wonderful and start cooing.

'Oh, blimey,' I say loudly. 'Forget my own head next!' Then, for the benefit of the people who've turned round to look at me, I add, 'Only forgotten my blooming case, haven't I?'

They turn away with expressions of distaste, and I beetle upstairs. Do it by the book. To my bedroom, pick up the suitcase, to the Long Gallery, down the 'Private' staircase. Out with the old metal-cutters, reach for the cables at the top of the alarm boxes, snip, snip. I'm tense then, but there's no noise.

Into the Great Hall, put the suitcase on the table. Unzip it all the way round, take the copy of the Madonna out of its cloth wrappings, and do what I have to do.

Slam the case shut, back up the stairs, Long Gallery, bedroom, back down the main staircase towards the hall, stop on the stairs, panting a bit. Whole operation – three and a half minutes.

Now you've probably gathered that I have got this unfortunate reputation for bogging things up. Just when the job's nearly done, something always seems to go wrong. Bad

luck I call it, but it's happened so often that some people have
less charitable descriptions.

So, anyway, there I am standing on the stairs in front of all
these people and I reach up to wipe my brow and – you'll never
believe it – I haven't had time to zip up my suitcase again and
I'm still holding the handle and it falls open. My aftershave and
what-have-you clatters down the stairs with my pyjamas, and
there, still strapped in the suitcase for all to see, is the Harbinger
Madonna.

'My God!' says Lord Harbinger.

I say a rude word.

Various servants come forward and grab me. Others are sent
off to the Great Hall to see the damage. Loxton's the first one
back. He looks dead peeved.

'My Lord. The alarm wires have been cut. He's replaced the
Madonna with a copy!'

'What!' Lord Harbinger blusters.

'Shall I call the police, my Lord?' asks another servant.

'Um . . .'

'All right.' I shrug. 'It's a fair cop. Story of my life. Every job
I seem to screw up. And this one I really thought I'd worked out
to the last detail.'

'Shall I call the police, my Lord?' the servant asks again.

'Um . . .'

'You better,' I say. 'I really have got caught with the goods
this time. I'm afraid the police are going to want a really
thorough investigation into this.'

'Ye-es.' His Lordship sounds uncertain. 'Under normal
circumstances of course I'd call the police straight away. But
this is rather . . . um . . . awkward.'

'Why?' I ask. 'I'm not pretending I haven't done it.'

'No, but, er . . . er . . .' Then finally he gets on the right
track. 'But you are a guest in my house. It is not part of the code
of the Harbingers to call the police to their guests, however they
may have offended against the laws of hospitality.'

'Oh,' I say.

'Gee,' says one of the Americans. 'Isn't this just *wonderful*?'

Harbinger's getting into his stride by now. He does a big point to the door like out of some picture and he says, 'Leave my house!'

I go down the rest of the stairs. 'Better not take this, had I, I suppose?' I hold up the Madonna.

'No.'

I hand it over, sort of reluctant. 'You better keep the copy. I got no use for it now. And I suppose the police will want to look at that. Might be able to trace back who ordered it.'

'Yes,' says his Lordship abruptly. 'Or rather no. You take that back with you.'

'But –'

'No. If the police could trace you through the copy, I would be offending the rules of hospitality just as much as if I had you arrested. You take the copy with you.'

'But I don't want it.'

'YOU WILL TAKE IT, SIR!' he bellows.

'Oh, all right,' I say grudgingly.

'Oh, heck. This is just so *British*,' says one of the Americans. Made her weekend, it had.

They give me the picture from the Great Hall, I put it in my suitcase, and I'm escorted out by Loxton. The punters and staff draw apart like I'm trying to sell them insurance.

Outside, Loxton says, 'God, I knew you were thick and incompetent, but it never occurred to me that you'd be *that* thick and incompetent.'

I hang my head in shame.

'Now get in your car and go!'

'Oh, it's not my car,' I say. 'It's stolen. Way my luck's going, I'll probably get stopped by the cops on the way home. I'll go on the coach to the station.'

Loxton doesn't look happy.

Takes a bit of time to get all the punters on to the bus. Loxton stands there fidgeting while further farewells are said. I sit right at the back with my suitcase. Everyone else sits right up the front. I'm in disgrace.

The bus starts off down the steep zigzag drive towards Limmerton. I look back to see Loxton rush towards the Peugeot, parked right in front of Harbinger Hall. I look at my watch. Quarter to seven. All that delayed us quite a bit.

I see Loxton leap into the car. Without bothering to close the door, he starts it and slams her into reverse. He screeches backwards over the gravel.

But it's too late. The Hall's saved, but he isn't.

The back of the Peugeot erupts into a balloon of orange flame. From inside the bus the sound is muffled. A few of the punters turn curiously, but just at that moment we swing round one of the hair-pins and there's nothing to see.

I piece it together again in the train. They've left me in a compartment on my own. I'm still like some kind of leper. They all feel better having had their guesses at the sort of person I was confirmed.

Lord Harbinger had money problems. Cost a lot to keep the Hall going, and the trippers weren't coming enough. Stately Home Weekends might bring in a few bob, but they took such a lot of staff, there wasn't much percentage in it.

But he had got the Madonna. Couldn't just sell it, wouldn't look good, public admission of failure. Besides, either he or Loxton had worked out a scheme that'd make more than just selling it. They'd have it stolen, get the insurance *and* sell it. But they need a real mug to do the actual thieving.

Enter Yours Truly.

I had to raise suspicions when I came for my day-trip, then stick out like a sore thumb on the Stately Home Weekend. When I'd actually done the theft, switched the real Madonna for the copy, Loxton would have offered to take my bag to my car. He would have switched my suitcase for the empty one and put the Madonna in another car, in which he would later drive it up to London to do his deal with Mr Depaldo's rival.

I would have driven off in the Peugeot, maybe full of plans to doublecross my paymasters and do a little deal of my own. They weren't worried what I had in mind, because they knew that half an hour away from Harbinger Hall, the dynamite in the back of the car would explode. When the police came to check the wreckage, I would be identified as the geyser who'd been behaving oddly all weekend, the one who'd obviously cut the alarm cables and switched the paintings. My profession was obvious. There was my record if they ever put a name to me. And if not, there were all the tools of my trade in the boot of the car.

Together with the dynamite, whose careless stowing caused my unfortunate demise.

And some burnt-out splinters of wood and shreds of canvas, which had once been a painting. A very old painting, tests would reveal. And the engraved brass plate which was likely to survive the blast would identify it as Giacomo Palladino's masterpiece, *Madonna and Child*. Another great art work would be tragically lost to the nation.

Had to admire it. Was a good plan.

They only got one thing wrong. Like a few others before them, they made the mistake of thinking Billy Gorse was as thick as he looked.

I felt good and relaxed. Pity the train hadn't got a buffet. I could have really done with a few beers.

Go to Red Rita's later, I thought. Yeah, be nice. Be nice to go away with her, and all. Been looking a bit peaky lately. She could do with a change. South America, maybe?

I got my suitcase down from the rack and opened it.

Found it grew on me, that Madonna.

And I was very glad I hadn't changed the two pictures round in the Great Hall.

I may not know much about art, but I'm beginning to realise what it's worth.

Lionel Davidson

I DO DWELL

He told me who he was and who the rest of them were, and he said I didn't have to be nervous. He said he knew it was distressing and they wouldn't keep me any longer than necessary. And I could have said it all for him. I mean, I read, I watch television. The twat was making me nervous just saying it.

There was a funny atmosphere in there anyway, floor polishy and official like school but not so farty. Like going in to the Head.

But I said what I had to. I knew it wasn't true but I said it. They'd taken me through it a few times, and they said not to *volunteer* anything, just tell the coroner what I'd seen, what I knew for a fact. Except I could say accident. I could say that, but only if it cropped up and in a natural way. Like they kept saying it naturally to me, accident, the accident. They were pretty damn sure it was suicide, only *I* wasn't supposed to know; not a little twat like me.

So he asked me how long I'd known Mr Sargent and I said eighteen months.

'Good friends were you, Miles, quite good chums, eh?'

'Yes, sir.'

'And you helped him a bit down there? With the chickens and horses and so on?'

'With Charlie, sir. Just the one horse.'

'Yes, Charlie. And you learned to ride him and shoot a bit, things like that?'

'Yes, sir.'

Shooting a bit. Things like that.

'About shooting. Mr Sargent was good with guns, was he?'

'Jolly good, sir.' Oh jolly, jolly.

'Tell us about the shot-gun. What he thought were the most important things you had to know.'

Oh well, God . . . The most important things I had to know, sir, were safety of the weapon and proper cleaning. Oh yes, awfully strict on cleaning, sir. Not *usually* pointed at himself while doing it, no, though occasionally I'd seen him do that; always after 'breaking' the gun first and checking that it wasn't loaded. He *was* sometimes absent-minded, yes, and on that occasion yes. Because of the interruption and the gun oil.

So we did all that. How he was taking me through the cleaning, when the phone rang and he said damn it, hang on a mo', and went and answered it. And then came back and started again, and realised he must have left the gun oil near the phone and could I nip in and get it. And how I couldn't see it there and had to look around, and while I was doing it heard the bang.

'What did you think then, Miles?'

'Nothing, sir. Not really.'

'You knew it was the gun.'

'I knew it was the gun, but I thought, I don't know, maybe he was – test-firing.'

'So what did you do?'

'I went on looking for the oil.'

'With no sense of alarm, nothing like that?'

'No, sir, not at all.'

'And when you didn't find the oil?'

'I went out to tell him, and I just – just saw him there.'

'Now, Miles. We know how you feel. I'm afraid you must tell us *exactly* what you saw.'

Sure, no sweat. Done it tons of times . . . He'd – he'd been sitting on the chopping block, sir. Where he did the logs and cleaned the gun. And I saw him, saw him . . . hanging sideways off it. With the gun on the ground as if he was reaching for it.

And the chickens cackling, and Charlie racing round the paddock. And I, I saw the side of his face. It was all so unreal I couldn't believe it. And I ran in and phoned my mother. And I didn't blub, sir, not till she turned up, sir.

'You've been a really good chap, Miles. Really very good and we won't keep you. But just one thing more. You know now that he had the gun oil on him all the time – that it was there in the pocket of his denim jacket?'

'Yes, sir.'

'So that with the interruption of the telephone call, his mind on other things, he was generally – absent-minded, would be your impression?'

'Yes, sir.'

'Very good. You've done well.'

Which I had and I sat and listened to the doctor and the police sergeant (one barrel fired, cleaning materials on the ground, position of gun consistent with accident); and not one more word about the phone call. I couldn't believe it. Well, I could. *They're so dopey*. They all are. But an Inquiry, for God's sake! And all of them sitting there *looking* so inquiring. Oh, hell. So they found he shot himself accidentally, while his mind was distracted, and we all got up and went. And I thought well they got that bit right anyway. His mind was definitely distracted when he came back out of the house. It was still the same way when I blew his head off. I don't know why I did it. I think it was to see really.

He came out and sat on the block and didn't say anything for a bit, and I said, Aren't we going to clean the gun, Humph? He said Yeah Miles, sure, we will, and looked over at the chickens and at Charlie, and he said I doubt your mother will be picking you up today Miles. I said OK – if I could take the bike? He let me take it the days she couldn't pick me up, and either she brought it back in the Range Rover or I just rode it when I came again. He said Sure, well, ah. We'll talk about it Miles, we'll do that, and looked all round again and then at his thumbs.

He didn't say any more, so I got the cleaning stuff ready and picked up the gun, already 'broken' on the canvas strip, and had a sniff, which I like. It wasn't loaded, but he had the cartridge box on the ground so I popped two in. I don't know why I did it. I just did. He was still looking at his thumbs but he half glanced up as he heard the breech snap and said, more or less automatically, Never point it Miles. Which actually I wasn't, I was just sighting it this way and that. But right then I wanted to. And I saw the angle was wrong, he was lower on the block. So I got down on one knee, Deadeye Dick, and pointed it. He said Look Miles, I've told you – and I squeezed and his face flew off. It was fantastic, it seemed to frizzle away, and he went backwards, blood and bits flying. And I stayed on my knee, seconds and seconds, not really able to believe what I'd done.

I felt like, electrocuted. I felt terrific. I felt really alive, and aware of every detail in the world. Like a flashlight photo – no, like a computer suddenly switching on a programme, all the stages, all the instructions. *Yes that is right, no that is wrong, go back to.* Charlie galloping and chickens cackling, yeah, but *he* was wrong. He'd put his arm out, but he'd have had them both out, he would have needed to, to steady the gun. It would have hit him like a train, sure, but with all his weight forward it wouldn't have knocked him right back. Sideways.

I yanked him up and he went sideways.

The bottle of oil fell out, and I thought about it and put it back in his pocket.

I got both arms right and scuffed the ground with the gun butt where it would have kicked, and got the gun right too. And on my hands and my sleeves blood, and I thought My God. I have just run out and found this terrible thing with Humph. I have touched him, and look half his face has gone and I am all over blood. What a terrible accident, I don't know what to do, I will phone my mother, my mother will know what to do. Oh my God, what a terrible thing for a boy to see.

But I didn't blub, not till the Range Rover tore up, and I did then, we both did, holding each other shocked and trembling, and she phoned the police. And she was looking at me all the time and licking her lips. But I was still shocked when the police came, so she said oh please can't it wait, and they said of course. So when Uncle Maurice came to the house later, about an hour later, he and my mother took me through it for the first time really, but carefully because of my blubbing, and as a lawyer he knows how to handle people.

Still, he said like, Did he mention who the phone call was *from* even? And I said no he didn't, which he hadn't; but he'd kept looking at the chickens, so maybe it was business, and perhaps I'd remember more later. And my mother: Maurice, I don't want him dwelling on it, please see they don't make him, it's too awful. And Uncle Maurice: of course, of course.

Well, he's a nice guy, maybe even too nice. No Range Rover for him, or anything like it, so perhaps he's a lousy lawyer. He's my mother's brother, he did her divorce, though it was 'pushing an open door' as he said. (My old man's in Saudi Arabia, he's making a fortune there.) All I know, when he took me through it later, again and again, the main thing on his mind was insurance, which I wasn't supposed to twig. I twigged it right off. Suicide was bad news, but an accident was OK and they'd pay. That, and no scandal. So it was accident, the accident. (But didn't he *think*? If it was suicide, would Humph have done it while I was there? I'm only a child, for God's sake.)

But the police didn't care, except for getting it all cleared up quickly, and neither did the coroner nor the dopey jury. So that was it, and nothing more about the phone call. And I thought, Are they all so dopey? Is everyone in the world? And can it always be so easy?

I kept thinking it, all during term, and sometimes it seemed sad because no more Humph and I couldn't help him again, and sometimes just comical. And at half term they told my mother I was taking it badly and maybe needed 'help'. (A shrink, see. I'd been found blubbing, and then laughing aloud for no reason.) Well, she wasn't having that. *I don't want him dwelling on it.* And she knew a shrink, anyway. So she said perhaps a short break, a little holiday somewhere.

So we had one. God, what a time for a holiday. Mid-winter. We went to the coast. We went to Eastbourne. Everywhere old shags in wheelchairs and these tea shops, and she didn't know what to do with me and hired me a bike. Which wasn't so bad really, in fact quite good. There are lots of places round there, and we put the bike in the back and went to them. A good one was the run near the lighthouse, just outside the town. There was a pub there where you parked the car, and crossed the road and went off up the grass. And she sat on the lookout seat while I scooted down – way down, turf all the way, dodging the rabbit holes and stones, sometimes with my feet on the crossbar, wow, really fast, maybe thirty, thirty-five miles an hour.

I had to push the bike back up, you couldn't ride it, but I usually got three or four goes in before she went out of her mind and also blue with cold just sitting at the lookout place. It's windy there, it always is, and she couldn't light a cigarette. She was smoking a lot of cigarettes. She was smoking right through meals, and in the bar (where I had to stay in a corner watching television while she sat on one of the tall seats). And then suddenly she wasn't, she'd cut down, and I wondered why, and one day spotted this guy Gerald. And I had a kind of sinking feeling because she was taking me for a twat again.

But I was really surprised. I thought she'd packed it in with Gerald. I thought she'd packed him in after Humph died. I knew about him – had known long before Humph, if Humph ever did know. And I knew it was somehow because of this Gerald that she'd phoned Humph that day. (Which was another thing. Didn't she *know* I knew? Because I hadn't blabbed did she think I was *such* a little twat?) And we just passed him there that day. He was sitting in a car, for Christ's sake, waiting. She slowed down as we passed, it was in this little village Alfriston, and pulled in to a pub car park beyond, and she said OK take an hour but not more, we have to be back for lunch, and I got the bike out and had this sinking feeling.

I started putting things together. We'd been here before, and it had happened before. And in the evenings she'd gone to bed early with a couple of aspirin in case of a cold that might be coming on, and not to bother looking in to say goodnight in case I woke her up.

Oh well, Jesus.

It was true she slept badly, but I suddenly saw this wasn't the reason we had two rooms, and that the little holiday wasn't just for me. And it made me sick, I mean after Humph and everything. A decent simple guy like Humph, and I'd been nervous for him right from the start, and couldn't bear the thought of him being unhappy. Because I knew she'd messed about with lots of. And it wasn't true my father was so keen on money and that's why he'd gone away for. It wasn't that at all, it was rotten being messed about and taken for a twat. It made me sick.

I didn't sneak back early, though. I took the hour, and she was finishing off a gin and looking quite good and it made me sick. And yeah I'd had a nice ride, and had a big appetite, and OK only one portion of pudding or I'd sink like a stone. (I went to the pool in the afternoons, they had a heated pool there.) But what was lousy was, this was a joke of my old man's, too much pudding and you'd sink like a stone. I mean, just because a person isn't there. Can you borrow them when you want? And can you give them back when you want? OK, I'm only a child and don't understand everything, but do they? Do they get cleverer as they get older, and know more? Or do they forget and go on doing all the same things because it's easier? Or even, can it be, that they do those things and only realise later why they've done them? Which is a thing that's been bugging me lately. But anyway I can't stand them being *tricky*, and rubbishing everything, and taking you for a twat. It makes me sick.

So anyway, lunch and the pool afterwards, and in the evening I said how about going to the pictures, we haven't been yet. (I didn't want her going off early, I really didn't want that.) But she said Oh great, all those people, sneezing and coughing away, and me trying so hard to keep a cold at bay. So OK, I watched television again, and she went off with a couple of aspirin, and I felt sick. And when I went up I thought *right in that next room* and I felt sick.

So in the morning I changed the routine, and did the pool first. Which she didn't want; she said much better the fresh air and having a blow. But I said no, the pool, so she got herself a magazine and an ashtray. (She wouldn't let me go in when she wasn't there. I mean, she really cared, I knew that; which didn't make it any better, it made it somehow sort of. Like as if I was a part of it; it was all in the family.) Then in the afternoon when we were going to this place Jevington, which we'd planned for the morning, which she'd then had to make a phone call about, which little twats weren't supposed to know, I said no I wanted the lighthouse.

Well, my God, scenes, she flipped. She said I was deliberately being bolshie, and half a gale was blowing and she'd be frozen. So I said OK, *you* don't have to come, and I can bike there and back, and what's such a big deal? But she wouldn't let me on my own, she said God above I'd drive her batty. And to stay where I was while she got a warmer coat and a scarf (yeah, and another bash at the phone). So we took off and she was fed to the teeth and crashing the gears and swearing.

And it *was* half a gale there, and she was muffled up, and we got the bike out and crossed the road and trudged up the hill, and she said Name of God, make it snappy, I'll turn to ice here. And boy, you could hardly stand up, and I was laughing, I really like it, it fills your mouth, it takes your breath away. She said You can have one go and come back by road, I'll wait in the car, I'm not waiting here.

But I wanted to see the waves first. Well, you couldn't see anything else – a huge mass of grey sea all streaked with white, and spray scudding – but I wanted to see them crash against the lighthouse. It's right below in the sea, five hundred feet below, the Beachy Head light. That's Beachy Head where I did my run.

She said Come back from there! You'll be blown off. But I yelled Don't worry, I'll be careful! and dropped the bike on the grass and crept to the edge, and I could see it then, we both could. It looked a toy lighthouse, striped red and white, and so far below it made you dizzy. Only the tide was still out so all you could see were tiny rocks, tiny, tiny. And the sound level was fantastic, a really colossal howl, and I couldn't stop laughing, and looked round, but there were no people to laugh with, not in that weather, and my mother couldn't stand heights and was just chattering with giddiness and cold. And as I looked round, she did too, as if maybe she expected someone, and I pushed.

She didn't see me; she didn't see anything really. And I didn't see her, not her face, not anything of her any more, just a big woolly toy, all curled up, going over. And again I could hardly believe it. It was incredible, so easy. And in all the wind even more unreal so I couldn't be absolutely certain it had happened.

But I didn't wait, not another moment. Got my bike and started the run, turf all the way, really terrific, the wind blowing me everywhere. And came to the bottom where it levels out before going down to the Birling Gap. Except I didn't continue. She said only one go, so I went back, by road as she said. And you couldn't even ride much of that, too hilly, so I was puffing and blowing as I got there again.

There was no one there, no one at the lookout place, so I took the bike across the road to the pub car park, and the Range Rover was there. Yeah, and another car, *that* one, way over to the side, and him sitting in it. I couldn't put the bike away, she had the keys, so I went to the pub, and it was closed, after hours. So I wandered over to him. He'd been watching me, over the top of his newspaper. He wound down the window and I said Excuse me, have you seen a – *hello*! And he said, Isn't it – is it Miles? And I said yeah, and what a funny thing, I was looking for my mother.

So we chatted a bit and he said where had I mislaid her, and I said she'd probably gone for a walk, she'd been frozen up there, and how I'd left her at the lookout place . . . Until the clot slowly took alarm and got out and started looking himself. And no joy from the pub, so we drove to the nearest phone box. And the police and the coastguards . . .

Well, I still didn't blub, not for a long time, not even after they assembled the tackle at the cliff edge. The tide had come in, so they couldn't manage from the shore. And they winched a guy down, and he was talking to them all the time on his bleeper, and it was when he said he could see her that I really started.

I mean it wasn't put on, it was real, it was hysterics. Like, No – oh no, please no! And moaning and dancing as if I was going to throw myself over. So they took me away, to a police station in Eastbourne. And it was policewomen and cups of tea, and a doctor saying I think a lie-down, and I'll just give him. And then, hours later, Uncle Maurice coming for me.

Except what I hadn't figured, the good bit, a guy with a dog had seen Gerald; had seen him earlier near the lookout place. So they gave him a bad time. Like taking him through everything, their meetings. And he'd been having rows with his wife, and she knew he was carrying on with somebody else and had told him to get rid of her. So all that was good and really screwed him up; and it wasn't even the end of it.

But I was terrible, awful, really depressed. And God, so lonely! I'd loved her and didn't know why I'd. I didn't have anybody now. I had Uncle Maurice and my father. He couldn't come for the funeral but he flew in a week later and said what did I want, and I didn't know. So Uncle Maurice said Give it time, we'll see, the poor kid has really had a. And for the time being he'll be with us. And the house going up for sale and everything, and a trust fund for me.

But God, awful, terrible, so lonely, and a stranger everywhere. Though they did everything for me, everything you could think of. Like shifting their kid Amanda out of her room so I wouldn't have to have the smaller one, and all my things could go in it. And Aunt Enid giving me lessons, she's a teacher, getting the right books and everything, so I wouln't have to go back just yet. But still feeling awful and lonely and depressed, like some lousy stinking illness that wouldn't ever go away. So in the end, God, a shrink.

Which nobody ever said, nor even mentioned. It was just another doctor who could help people at times like these. But Christ I knew, and I was scared. I mean I read, I watch television. It's not what you say to them. It's what they. And they're all tricky. And this one was, and right away I didn't like him. So kind, and understanding, and what the hell was it he was understanding?

Like we started off with just changing pills, I was having pills. And this one was a little too strong, wasn't it, and left me drowsy in the morning, which made lessons a bit tough, didn't it, old chap? So we'd try this, and then maybe at times when I felt *very* down in the dumps, this one would help. And if we could find a *pattern* for these times, we could adjust the doseage so I needn't go through the rotten business at all. And might a bit of riding buck me up again?

Which was another thing: riding. They must have told him about Charlie, because I hadn't, but he knew, and kept giving me bits of news to cheer me up. Like, Charlie was turning into a first-class coal-heaver now. (A farmer was looking after him. Humph's old place was up for sale, and the chickens had been sold, but Charlie was doing odd jobs for this farmer who had another horse and didn't mind; and he'd been pulling a fuel cart to their coal-fired greenhouses.)

So I said, well maybe, I didn't know yet. And he said he'd run me round one day to see him. And I mustn't feel gloomy about old Humph. Accidents happened, and life was often messy but that was how it was and we couldn't tidy it up even though we'd like to. Which was another thing that bugged me; the way he often echoed what I was thinking myself, but all dead cheery and sensible and mainly just as he was going.

And he took us both, Amanda and me, and Charlie knew me and came over right away, and I didn't have any Polo mints. But this guy did, the doctor, can you beat it. He said he had them to stop smoking. Only Charlie wouldn't take them from him, only me. Well, and from Amanda too, which I didn't like so I didn't give him any more. And it was right he was sucking them to stop smoking, in the car, but I hadn't seen him doing it before, and thought damn it, how could he know about Charlie and Polo mints? Uncle Maurice didn't know and nobody knew. So maybe it *was* only to stop smoking, but.

And then again with Amanda. Like, I was making out she was my little sister now – my dear little five-year-old. And she definitely thought I was her big brother, and *wanted* me to have her room, she really did. So where did he get it that I really thought she was a tricky little creep who would make trouble for me one day?

I don't know where he got it. He never even said it. He did it with his eyebrows, or his eyes, rolling them, one time when she just left the room. And I wondered if she'd said or done something I hadn't caught. But she hadn't, she hadn't said anything, just grinning and showing me a ballpoint of mine she'd found that I'd lost behind the desk, and putting it back where I could see it. So I thought maybe I was imagining it, but I knew I wasn't. I didn't like him. He was tricky.

Like with the dreams. He said he'd heard that with these pills some people dreamed more, and did I? And I said no, not really, not that I could remember. He said it would be quite normal after all I'd gone through, nature's way, part of the healing process, and I shouldn't try and block them. In fact it would be an idea if I tried to retain them and tell him the bits I remembered.

So I said OK and made up a few (if it was so normal, if it was expected), though I knew he was being tricky somehow. And they were just ordinary kind of dreams that I knew everybody had, like falling, which seemed a good idea anyway, and being lost in a maze, and being trapped, and he made notes and pretended to be dead interested, and maybe he was.

But Christ I *was* having dreams, and maybe it was the pills. And they frightened the hell out of me, but not in any normal way. Like I'd just murdered someone, no one in particular, no one I could remember, and I'd got a terrific kick out of it. And either they'd done something rotten, or they'd be better off if, or anyway everything would be neater. But it was what I did right after that was great, like proving it wasn't me, and changing things so none of the twats could see or even find something I'd just used. Which was really exciting, everything happening very fast, and I'd wake up still alert and tingling all over.

Then I'd slowly realise, and still feel myself excited, and that's what frightened me. I mean I'd felt it all before, and I knew what happened before and how I'd felt sick and terrible later. But still I felt the excitement now, and liked it, and wanted it, and thought Oh God no, don't let me.

But of course I didn't tell him these, and the ones I gave him seemed OK, and he said Yes well, Miles, we're going forward, we're going forward, we might have got the dosage right now. Which I think he had. I wasn't drowsy in the mornings any more, and the hellish empty feeling didn't come so often. And I was biking again, and going off to the farm to see Charlie. And then this ghastly stinking awful day.

I'd just come back from Charlie, it was tea-time, and they were all in a flap. And Aunt Enid in a cocktail dress, and her hair, and they were going off to a cocktail party miles away, and the baby sitter had cancelled. And Jesus, phoning around and getting nowhere, and Uncle Maurice: Enid, it'll be perfectly all right, he's a responsible boy and we'll only be gone a few hours. I felt sick and frightened and couldn't think what to say. I mean, what could I say?

So they gave her her tea and said she had to be a good girl and do what Miles said. And Aunt Enid said to let her play in the playhouse for half an hour and to stay with her there (there was this playhouse in the garden); and just before they left, quietly to me: She'll want drinks of water and so on, but don't let her get away with it. Let her just do her colouring in bed, and you watch the television and she'll go off to sleep.

67

Oh well God, I was trembling and I didn't want it, and prayed they'd come back early because I couldn't trust. And they said they would, as early as they could, by nine anyway. So goodbye goodbye and we played in the rotten playhouse for half an hour. And went in, and I said bed now, and she said I had to undress her. So I wouldn't let her get away with that (God!) and said she was a big girl now and I'd really think she was very clever if she did it herself and I bet she couldn't get her pye-jies on, not all by herself. Which thank Christ she did.

So I got her in, and read to her for a bit, and said OK she could do some colouring now and I was going down. And she had to have everything just as she wanted it, her bits of paper and colouring stuff here, and Teddy there, and the curtains not quite closed, and the door left open.

But I did it all and went and switched the TV on, and blow me down, ten minutes later she was yelling for a drink of water. Which I put up with for a bit, and then couldn't stand any more and went and got her one. And she said stay with her for just a bit, and I said no she had to go to sleep now, and took the papers away and switched the light off. But I shut the door too, and she started howling right away, Don't close it, don't close it, I can't open it; which was true, she couldn't, it stuck. So I opened it a crack, and she thought of something else. Teddy was frightened, he was a terrible baby, and he wanted the night light.

So damn it, I had to do that too, and went to the kitchen for the matches, and on the way back up thought of it and started trembling. I thought Oh God no, please not, I don't want to. I don't want to even think of it. And I knew I had to get out of the room fast, which I did. I said, Don't call any more, I'm not listening, go to sleep now, OK?

And went down and turned the sound up so I wouldn't hear her if she called. I really didn't want to do it. I didn't want to. But at the same time I did. I could see it all. The night light flickering, and one of the papers catching. And the door stuck so she couldn't open it, and flames and smoke. And me not smelling it till I went out to see if she was all right, and little wisps of smoke, the door jammed, and. And her out of the way first, of course. A pillow or something. Or could they tell if a person was already? But I'd think of something, I knew I would, and getting more and more excited.

And really trembling and hardly able to sit there, so I concentrated as hard as I could on, I think it was a pop show, with strobe lights. But I heard her all the same, Miles, Mi-iles, and turned it up even louder. And practically jumped right out of my skin when she said it in my ear. She was there. She'd come down! She was standing there in her pye-jies, with Teddy.

I said, What is it? What are you doing here?

She said she wanted wee-wees.

I said, Well go and have one.

She said someone always went with her.

I said not this time, she was a big girl and she could go on her own. But she said she couldn't pull the handle, so I said I'd pull it later, and she started crying.

So Christ, I was trembling all over, and I said OK I'd do it, and we went up together, and I had to hold one of Teddy's arms while she held the other. And I was still fighting very hard, and I said she had to be quick and I'd wait outside. But no, I had to go in with her, and I suppose I could have stopped that, I could have said no, though it was something about the seat being too high, but I needn't. But I knew I'd had it now, I just knew it, and couldn't stop myself.

And yeah, she started showing off, showing me her thing, I knew she would, she'd done it at bath-time, it makes me sick. And my heart was thudding, because I knew I was going to do it. And at the same time sick and frightened because wasn't it too much of a coincidence, and what would they think, or would they think a jinx? And could I get it burning properly, the bed-clothes and everything, and how long would it?

So she finished and I pulled the handle, and she said tuck her in, and I said OK. And I got her in, and Teddy, and she was only little and I thought Christ. So I kissed her goodnight again and was practically sick all over her, I could feel it rising in my throat. And while I was doing it, whipped the pillow out from under her and got it over her face and she started wriggling about, and I tried hard to keep the vomit down and pressed hard, and it was all unreal again, as unreal as before, and I was floating, flying, flying through the air. And landing in a heap on the floor the other side of the room. And before I could pick myself up, before I could even figure out what was happening, Uncle Maurice had taken the pillow off and Gerald was coming in the room.

And I was being sick, on the carpet, on my knees; at the same time understanding it, though, all at once. I've always been very quick. The wardrobe door still open, where Uncle Maurice had stepped out of it; and not only Gerald, but the doctor also coming in. Yeah, and these last two, sitting on each side of me, on my bed. But I'd seen it all, had understood it all, before they told me.

Play with her in the playhouse for half an hour, while they went off. Yeah, and while they came back! So they'd been there all the time, three of them staked out in the house and watching me (but not Aunt Enid, she came in after they got me). And Gerald – the shrink my mother had known. And him being suspicious of Humph's case right from the start, and for the reasons I'd thought up myself. *Not* suicide, because why would he while I was there, only a child for God's sake? But *only* an accident, after that phone call, which he'd known about, had known who it was from, what it was about? And had kept quiet about because he was involved himself. And had grown interested in me. And heard the reports of me at school, and the little holiday and everything. And had kept an eye on me. And knew my mother hated heights and wouldn't go near the cliff edge herself, and wasn't suicidal in any way.

So his friend, his colleague, who could 'help people at times like these' . . . Yeah, and who understood so much about me, echoing my thoughts before I knew them myself. And Amanda, and Polo mints for Charlie.

So here I am, and I don't like this place. And I told you right away, my mother didn't want me to dwell on anything. She must have told *him*, and he'll have told you, so what else do you want from me? OK, I'm not very well, and I'll dwell if you think it will help, but what's going to happen to me now?

Michael Gilbert

A VERY SPECIAL RELATIONSHIP

On a Thursday in July the Brentwood branch of the National Bank opened its doors at the normal hour of 9.30. At 9.31 a car drew up on the other side of the High Street and four men got out, strolled across the road and went into the Bank.

Young George Williamson, the bank clerk on duty at the counter nearest to the door, thought that he had never seen four such odd customers. His first reaction was amusement. They looked, he thought, like a quartet of amateur actors. Extras, in some country house scene, who would be found, when the curtain went up, strolling about up-stage, murmuring 'Rhubarb' to each other. One, who looked the youngest, had blond hair, one had brown hair, one had red hair and the largest of the four had black hair. All of them had moustaches which exactly matched their hair and the big man sported, in addition, a neat black beard.

As they walked through the door the impression of chorus work was increased as each of them whipped out and put on a pair of dark glasses.

Fear came when the blond young man produced an automatic pistol from inside his coat and said, in conversational tones, 'If you or your muckers make any move I don't like, I'm going to open up your stomach. Tell the other two geezers to move up here.'

For a moment Williamson was paralysed with shock. He saw the gun come up and waved frantically. The other two tellers, both older men, sidled along towards Williamson.

'Lovely. Now you can all sit down and hold hands. Don't be bashful. Fact is, I feel more comfortable if I can see where your hands are. That's right. Now you be good boys and you won't be hurt.'

Meanwhile brown hair had taken a chair and set himself down beside the street door. He had a shot-gun across his knees. The commissionaire lay on the floor behind him. Blood was trickling slowly from a wound on his forehead and dribbling down onto the polished floor.

The other two men had walked straight across into the manager's office. Mr Pilkington was behind his desk, opening the morning mail, with his secretary in a chair beside him. He jumped up, knocking over his own chair as he did so.

The big man said, 'Don't let's waste time, dad. All you have to do is open up the strong-room and fetch out the cash. Thursday's pay day round here I understand, so there'd better be plenty of it. And no tricks.'

Both men had produced sacks which they must have been carrying, rolled up, inside their coats.

The manager said, 'I can't –' but got no further. Red hair, who had worked his way round behind the desk hit him a slashing blow across the face which threw him back against the wall. The big man said, 'If you don't do what I say, and quick, I'm going to blow this girl's face in, and don't think I'm joking.'

The manager said, 'All right.' He spoke with difficulty. The blow had split his lip and broken two teeth. With a hand that was shaking he got a ring of keys from his pocket and unlocked the door in the panelling which led down to the strong-room.

'She comes with us,' said the big man.

In less than ten minutes they were back again. Both sacks were bulging. The girl carried one, red hair the other.

'Now show me the way out at the back,' said the big man.

The manager led the way out into a passage at the end of which was a strong looking door.

The big man said, 'Unlock it.'

'It's bolted, not locked,' said the manager thickly.

'Then unbolt it.'

As the manager stooped to the bottom bolt the big man kicked him. The boot caught him under the chin. There was a crack as the jaw bone splintered. The manager tumbled into a heap on the floor.

The big man was already moving back towards the office. Red hair had finished tying the girl to her chair and was now gagging her. He said, 'Seems they've got company out front.'

The big man opened the door and looked into the bank. Three men and two women were squatting on the floor behind the door. Brown hair, who was sitting astride his chair beside them, said, 'We may have trouble.'

'What sort of trouble?'

'Another man looked in just now. Dodged out before I could stop him.'

'All right,' said the big man. 'We've finished.'

Three of them moved back into the office. The blond boy stepped up to the street door and eased it open. Two policemen were standing beside the Ford Escort.

'Bastards,' said the young man. As slowly and carefully as though he was firing at a target on the range, he took aim and squeezed the trigger. The nearer of the two policemen jack-knifed forward as the heavy bullet hit him in the spine. The second one grabbed him as he fell and started to pull him round behind the car.

'Easy meat,' said the young man. He took aim and fired again. The second man jerked, but continued to pull. Both of them were now lying behind the car.

The blond boy turned back into the bank, smiling broadly. Everyone there was frozen into shocked immobility. He said, 'If anyone moves for the next two minutes, he gets the same.' Then he walked into the manager's office and shut the door behind him.

Williamson was already crawling across the floor behind the counter. One of the older assistants tried to stop him. He said, 'You heard him. Two minutes, he said.'

'Be your age,' said Williamson. He reached the alarm and pressed it.

Outside, at the back and a little distance away, they heard a car starting up.

Chief Superintendent Morrissey, the big white-faced Jew, had boxed for the police in his youth. He was heavier and slower now, but still formidable. He had summoned the heads of the four North London Special Crime Squads to his room at New Scotland Yard.

He said, 'This business at Brentwood. We haven't got much yet. In fact, to be perfectly accurate, we've got bugger all. I couldn't talk to the manager. He's in hospital having his jaw set and is still under sedation. The commissionaire's OK, but he was put out almost as soon as the men got inside. All he knows is that the man who hit him had brown hair – and dark glasses. The girl's been having hysterics on and off ever since. Two of the clerks saw the one they call "the young man" quite clearly. So clearly, that all they can tell us about him is that he had light hair – and dark glasses.'

Superintendent Tim Collinson, the head of No. 1 Squad, was tempted to make a comment, but he refrained. He thought that he had rarely seen the old man angrier.

'The only one who kept his head and kept his eyes open –' Morrissey was looking at the papers on the table '– was the youngest of the clerks. Name of George Williamson. It seems he does a bit in the acting line himself. He says that all the men were wearing wigs, but that he could see enough of the young man's hair, which was rather long, to tell that his own hair was, in fact, very light. He thought that the older man, the one who seemed to be the leader, had grey hair.'

He looked down again at the paper.

'All the moustaches and the beard, he thought, were false. From which we could assume that in real life the men are clean-shaven. They had been made-up in quite a professional way, eye lines, eyebrows and so on. Brown hair, who carried the shot-gun, had had a couple of teeth blacked out and red hair had a noticeable scar on the side of his face. Almost certainly phoney.'

'Then the only thing we know about them,' said Collinson, 'is that one of them must be a dab hand at amateur theatricals.'

'They wouldn't have made the wigs themselves,' said one of the other men. 'They'd have bought them from a theatrical costumier. Might be a line there.' He didn't sound very hopeful.

'We know something else about them,' said Morrissey. He spoke with unusual venom. 'One of them is a cold-blooded young shit. There was no sort of reason to shoot those two men. They'd just arrived on the scene and were examining the car. The male chorus had finished their act and were on the way out. They had a second car parked two streets away. They were in no sort of danger. But blondie had to demonstrate his skill with a gun. Which cost us Courtauld dead and Mathieson with a bullet through the top of his thigh. He may lose that leg. Until these men are caught, no one's safe. So we've got to catch them.'

There was a pause whilst he organised his thoughts. He said, 'We'll run it through No. 1 Squad. That puts you in charge, Tim. But you can call on any help you want from other Squads. My guess would be that black hair is the organiser. He probably scouts the job himself. Respectable looking grey-haired number, he could walk into any bank and chat up the manager. Maybe he's the make-up artist too. Got the stuff in his own house. Then all he's got to do is whistle in the other three, explain the scenario and off they go.'

'They picked up a hundred and twenty thousand in notes on the Brentwood job,' said Collinson. 'Should keep them happy for a while.'

'Agreed,' said Morrissey. 'The next job won't be next week, or even next month. That gives us time. Spread the word down the grass-roots. All normal rewards for information are doubled. And of course, if one of the four should decide to talk he gets a complete indemnity, as well as the reward that's been put up by the bank. One other thing. You can tell all your men, from me, that if they catch them on the job, they don't mess about. This time, they shoot first. Best is aim for their legs and keep on shooting till they go down. If there are any complaints, I'll carry the can. I'd rather see four of them crippled than lose two more good men like Courtauld and Mathieson. Is that clear?'

They agreed that it was clear.

It was just after ten o'clock on a Friday evening in the last week of August when the four men came to Number Ten, Roberts Road. They approached it from behind, climbed the wall at the end of the garden and made their way up the grass path to the kitchen quarters at the back of the house. One of the men broke a pane of glass in the scullery door, put in a gloved hand and turned the catch. The four men walked in through the kitchen and into the front hall. Their rubber-soled shoes made very little noise, but it would be incorrect to suggest that they walked stealthily. They carried themselves like men who were masters of the situation.

They stopped outside the drawing-room door. There was light under it and they could hear the sound of music.

'Just the two of them, I guess,' said the big man with the black beard. 'Listening to the telly. Where do you think the kids are?'

'Tiny tots wouldn't be sitting up at this time of night,' said the blond young man.

'Tucked up in their little beds upstairs,' agreed red hair. 'Bless their sweet hearts.'

They had not troubled to lower their voices. The sound of music broke off abruptly and footsteps approached the door. As it was opened, the big man kicked it. It swung back, knocking the man behind it onto the floor. As he fell his glasses came off. He groped for them blindly for a moment, found them and scrambled to his feet; a tubby little man in his middle forties. His face registered blank astonishment as he looked at the quartet.

'You're speechless,' said the big man. 'Quite right. When you don't know what to say, don't say anything.'

He spared a glance for the woman who was sitting in the chair beside the television set; and looked a second time with appreciation. Twenty years younger than her husband, he guessed. And quite a looker.

He said to her, 'Turn the telly on again, darling. We'd like a little background music. Let's all sit down, shall we? That's right. Now I want to start by making one or two things clear. Do you happen to know Pilkington, Mr Laybourne?'

'The manager of our Brentwood branch. Yes, I know him.'

Mr Laybourne had got his voice back and a little of his self possession.

'Of course. All you senior managers know each other. That's natural. I wondered if you'd seen him lately?'

'I visited him in hospital.'

'Was he talking again?'

'Not very much.'

'It's an unpleasant thing, a broken jaw,' said the big man thoughtfully. 'Painful at the time and awkward afterwards. Difficult to eat or talk. Specially if you happened to lose some of your teeth too.'

Since this seemed to require some comment Mr Laybourne said, 'Yes, I expect it is.'

'You're wondering why I should be telling you this. You see that telephone by your chair. There's one in the hall, too. And another one, perhaps, upstairs in your bedroom.'

Mr Laybourne nodded.

'Now you may have thought that we should put these telephones out of action. Cut the wires, smash the instruments. It's what villains do in books. But we think a bit further ahead. Suppose one of your friends wants to get in touch with you. Dials your number. No answer. That's odd, they think. They might report it to the Post Office. Or if they live nearby they might come round to see what's up. No, no. Much better leave the telephones alone. Then, if they ring up, you can answer them and they can hear your cheerful voice agreeing to play golf tomorrow. You do play golf?'

'Yes, but I don't see –'

'You don't follow the logic of what I'm saying. Let me explain. If you didn't answer, cheerfully and happily, or if you or your wife was so stupid as to think you might use one of those telephones to call for help, then two of us would hold you and I'd break your jaw up with a hammer. Then you could have the pleasure of watching while we did the same to your wife. Maybe we'd have time to attend to the children as well.'

Mr Laybourne had gone white, but he still had command of his voice. He said, 'I can assure you we shall behave sensibly. And the children aren't here. They're spending the weekend with their grandmother.'

'Excellent. Then we understand each other. And when you say you'll be sensible, I take it you're speaking for your wife as well. Or has she got some different opinions?' He turned to look at the woman. She was certainly worth looking at. He said, 'Since we'll be spending some time together, darling, why don't we loosen up a little. For a start, I take it you've got a Christian name.'

'My name's Susan. And I agree with what my husband said.'

'Then what about getting us all a cup of coffee, Susan.'

That was the beginning of a very long night.

At midnight the lights in the drawing-room and front hall were turned off and they all moved into the back kitchen. Brown hair was despatched upstairs. 'Bathroom lights, thirty minutes. Bedroom lights, another quarter of an hour,' the big man decreed. 'That about right? Or do you read in bed?'

'No.'

'Better things to do, eh, Susie,' suggested the blond boy with a grin.

Susan ignored this. She said to the big man, 'If we're going to sit up all night, I could cut some sandwiches.'

'Good idea. And put on a bit more coffee. It'll stop us going to sleep.'

Twice more, during that interminable night, she handed out cups of coffee. No one tried to sleep.

At seven o'clock Susan started preparations for breakfast. The big man said, 'Time we all smartened ourselves up. We'll use the bathroom in turns. Red goes up first with Mr Laybourne. And go easy with that scar of yours, Red, when you're shaving.'

Red hair, who seemed to be the most amiable of the four, grinned and led the way up to the bathroom.

'Must look tidy for the next part of the programme,' said the big man. Over breakfast he lined it up for them. He said, 'The bank's shut on Saturday, but twice in the past month you've been there on Saturday morning with a couple of other men. Smart types, with big brief cases. Got there about ten o'clock and left at lunch-time. Right?'

'That was when the audit was being done. It's finished now.'

'Wrong,' said the big man. 'They found they'd added up one of the columns wrong. They're going back this morning to check. Fetch the gear up from the car, Brownie.'

Brown hair departed down the garden and came back with a large suitcase. From it he extracted two brief cases, two pairs of striped trousers, two neat buff-coloured raincoats and two black Homburg hats. When red hair and brown hair had dressed up, the big man inspected them as though they had been soldiers on parade. He said, 'Keep the raincoats buttoned up until you're inside and you should pass muster. Better still if you were carrying rolled umbrellas as well as brief cases, but you may need to have a hand free. And for God's sake, Red, put that hat on straight. Respectable accountants don't walk round with their titfers on one side of their heads. OK. Off you go. Mr Laybourne will drive you down in his car. You usually park it in the alley-way alongside the bank, don't you? Some arrangement with the police, I believe.'

If Mr Laybourne was surprised at the knowledge of his habits which the big man seemed to have acquired he did not show it. He seemed, by now, to be almost resigned.

'When you get there, Mr Laybourne gets out and opens up the side door of the bank. Red goes with him. Brownie, you turn the car round. Then go in after them.' He looked at his watch. 'Half-past nine. If I don't hear from you by half-past ten, I'll start worrying. And when I start worrying, I start getting active.'

Back in the drawing-room the big man and Susan settled down to wait. The boy seemed unable to sit still. They could hear him moving about upstairs. The big man had his chair placed so that he could look out of the window without being seen. He was sitting quite still, but she could feel the tension building up inside him. This was the climax, the bad hour when there was nothing for either of them to do but wait. Both of them were hoping that nothing would go wrong at the bank. Community of feeling was building a curious bond between them.

'It should be all right,' said the big man, as though he were reading her thoughts. 'You husband's behaved very sensible so far. No reason he should spoil it now.'

Susan said, 'He hadn't much choice, really, had he?' She realised that he wanted to talk and seemed happy to oblige him.

'No choice,' said the big man. 'But that doesn't stop people making fools of themselves. Mind you, I wasn't too surprised. Your husband's a senior and experienced man. No. It's you who's been the real surprise.'

'You think I ought to have had hysterics, perhaps?'

'I've known women do that. Hold one of them at the end of a gun and you can't tell how she'll react. Sometimes they cry. Sometimes they go frozen and dumb. Sometimes it's quite the opposite. They want to make love to you.'

'I don't believe it.'

'It's true though. When you come to think about it, it's a very special relationship between a man with a gun, who's ready to use it, and someone who's at the other end of the gun. Think about it. All the time we've been here, from the very first we've been bosses and you two have been our servants. Slaves almost, you might say.'

'You think some women like being dominated?'

Susan sounded coolly interested.

'Most women like to be dominated.'

'Maybe. But I can't see anything out of the ordinary about pointing a gun at someone and making them do what you want.'

'That's because you're at the wrong end of the gun. If you were holding it in your hand, you'd realise exactly what I mean.'

'Suppose we try the experiment.'

'I think not,' said the big man with a smile. 'You're too damned cool. You'd probably pull the trigger. But take a weak character like Blondie, who's fiddling round upstairs because his nerves won't let him sit still. Put a gun in his hand, and he's a great big he-man. Take his gun away and he's a scared kid. The gun's his prick, sort of.'

'His – ?'

'I beg your pardon. I'd forgotten we were in the upper echelon. I should have said his genital organ.'

'Oh yes. I read about that theory somewhere. Actually I concluded that the author was an amateur psychologist and was talking through his hat.'

'Don't you believe it. Why, I can tell you –' Before he could tell her anything he was interrupted.

There was a clatter of footsteps on the stairs and the blond boy arrived. He seemed to have something on his mind. He said, 'It's the first time I've been into some of those other rooms. And what do you think I found in the room at the end of the passage?'

'A dozen armed policemen,' suggested the big man.

'I found the bed made up and all her things by it. If she's his wife, why isn't she sleeping with him?' His voice was sharp with suspicion.

Susan said, 'I assume from that, that you're a bachelor.'

'What's it got to do with it?'

'If you were a married man you'd know that there comes a time – every three or four weeks – when it's not very comfortable for a man to sleep with his wife.'

'Doctors call it a period,' said the big man kindly. 'Women call it the curse.'

'How do we know she's telling the truth – about that or anything? She's too damned smooth. I'll tell you what, though–' his tongue came out and passed over his lips. He looked absurdly young, Susan thought. Like a small boy who's been promised a cream cake. 'We could always find out. Tell her to take her pants off.'

'We could,' said the big man. 'But we're not going to. Because if we did and if things happened to go wrong, a charge of attempted rape would be thrown in for good measure and that would add an extra five years onto what the judge dished out.'

The young man pouted. He said, 'Have it your own way, boss, but I think there's something screwy about her.' He was moving round the room as he spoke. 'I'll tell you another thing I noticed. There's lots of photographs, in the bedroom and down here–' he picked up the framed photographs of a boy and a girl which stood on the mantelpiece between the clock and a jar of rather wilted chrysanthemums. 'There's pictures of the two kids. There's pictures of dogs and horses and one of old Laybourne, all dressed up and making a speech to a lot of other old geezers – but not one, not a single bloody solitary photograph of her. Does that seem natural?'

He was answered by a shrill summons from the telephone.

'Get out into the hall and listen in,' said the big man. And, to Susan, 'You take the call in here.'

It was a woman's voice. She said, 'Susan? Margaret here. I hope this wasn't an awkward moment to ring up. Something on the boil or you in your bath?'

'Nothing like that,' said Susan. 'I was sitting in the drawing-room like a perfect lady, thinking about life.'

'Lucky you. Well I'm afraid I've got a disappointing bit of news for you. Both the kids are down. Some sort of virus. Nothing dangerous, the doctor says. I was a bit anxious last night, because Simon was a hundred and one and Anita was well over a hundred, but they've gone down now. And they've got their appetites back.'

'That's always a good sign.'

'But I'm afraid we'll have to call off the tea party we'd fixed for Wednesday. Will you break it to your two?'

'I'll tell them as soon as they get home on Monday. And don't worry, Margaret. Children's temperatures go up and down like a yo-yo.'

The woman said, 'Bless you,' adding softly, 'And the best of luck.' Then she rang off.

'Now what did she mean by that?' said Blondie, bursting back into the room. 'Why did she wish *you* good luck? It's not *your* children who are ill.'

Susan, who had taken the telephone call standing up, had now returned to her chair. Her hands were along the arms of the chair and the big man saw her knuckles go white for an instant as she tightened her grip.

Then she said, slowly, 'I imagine she wished me good luck because she knew that the next ten minutes would be tricky. Let me explain. When she said, "both the kids are down" it meant that both your men had been taken. When she added that they'd got their appetites back it meant that there'd been no casualties. Well, that was good news, though it wasn't unexpected.'

'If that's true,' said Blondie thinly, 'it means there's going to be another casualty, right here.' He swung round on the big man, 'Do you think she's telling the truth?'

'You can test it,' said Susan. 'You'll have noticed that I haven't looked out of the window since I came in here. If you look now you should be able to see a green van at one end of the road. Not actually blocking the road, but drawn into the side and ready to pull out. There'll be a much larger one, it looks like a laundry delivery van, at the other end of the road.'

Blondie shifted the net curtain and peered out.

'The vans are there all right. So what's the score?'

'If Morrissey is operating on his usual scale, it means that he's got a dozen men in position in front of the house and the same number behind it.'

There was a long silence. Blondie said, rather desperately, 'What do we do? Maybe we could use her as a shield.'

'A bit small to cover both of us,' said the big man. He still seemed unruffled. 'Before we do anything stupid, there's one thing I'd like to find out. You said just now that you'd *expected* them to pick up Red and Brownie without any fuss. No casualties, you said. Why were you so confident?'

'The cards were stacked against them,' said Susan. 'We knew exactly when to expect them and what they were going to do.'

'Right. I thought that was what you meant. And I found it surprising. I'm a very cautious operator. We'd had Mr Laybourne watched, discreetly. The general idea was there, but no one except me knew just how we were going to play it. And what's more important, no one but me knew when the kick-off was going to be. That right Blondie?'

'That's right,' said Blondie. He spoke so thickly that they could hardly make out the words. Something seemed to have gone wrong with his face.

'I gave everyone their marching orders at my place on Thursday night. *Until then no one knew the details except me.* And after that we were together all the time until we came here.'

'All the time?' said Susan softly. The words hung in the silent room.

'Well,' said the big man, almost as though he was speaking to himself. 'Let me think about that. Red and Brownie, certainly. But it occurs to me –'

He swivelled round and looked directly at Blondie.

'Was there something?' said Blondie. There was a touch of the old bravado in his voice, but it no longer sounded convincing.

'Now that I think about it – yes. Of course.'

'What are you talking about?'

'You were the only one who wasn't with us all the time. After I'd explained it all to you, you slipped out didn't you? To telephone your girl, I think you said.'

Susan said, 'Might that, perhaps, have been about eleven o'clock?'

'About then. Why?'

'I do know that it was about then that Morrissey got the tip-off. I remember the time because there was a lot to arrange. We none of us got much sleep that night.'

'It's a fucking lie.' Blondie's voice had gone up nearly into the treble pitch. 'A fucking bloody lie.'

'No,' said the big man. 'No. Keep your hands where they are.' His own hand had slid into the front of his jacket and came out holding a Colt Python. 'Now you can pull your gun out. But pull it out slow. Keep it pointed down. That's right. Now drop it on the floor.'

Deprived of his gun, the blond boy seemed to disintegrate before their eyes. Take his gun away, the big man had said, and he's just a scared kid. He was a scared kid now all right, thought Susan.

'Of course,' said the big man, 'it might have been a coincidence. Coincidences do happen. He might have gone out to phone his girl friend.'

'I did. I swear I did,' said the boy. 'Don't believe a word she says. It's a frame-up. A fucking bloody frame-up.'

'At the same time,' said the big man dispassionately, 'there is the fact that somehow our exact timetable got leaked to the fuzz. Could have been telepathy, I suppose.'

Susan said, 'It occurs to me that there's one way of finding out if Blondie here is playing on our side.'

'Then let's have it.'

'Don't listen to her.'

'Why not?' said the big man. 'She says there's an easy way of finding out which side you're on. OK. Let's find out.'

'When we were given our instructions,' said Susan, 'Morrissey said something to us. It was because he was so angry about what had happened at Brentford.'

As she said this she shot a quick glance at Blondie. His disintegration was almost indecent. His eyes were flickering, his lips were twitching and there was a trickle of saliva at each corner of his mouth. 'It wasn't my fault.' The words tumbled out. 'We all had guns. We were told to shoot.'

'I thought at the time you were a bit impulsive,' said the big man judgematically. 'Clever shooting, but not strictly necessary. So what had Chief Superintendent Morrissey got to say about it?'

'I think he imagined that all four of you were gun happy, like this kid. So he said this. It was an order. If we found ourselves up against your lot there was to be no hanging back. We were to shoot first and shoot fast. Not to kill. Aiming at the legs. I think perhaps he meant the word to get round. He thought one of you might be scared enough at the prospect to come across.'

'The old bastard,' said the big man. 'So that was his idea, was it? I can believe it, too. He's no gentleman.' He swung round on Blondie. 'So now we've got two things to thank you for, kiddo. First you leak the job. Then you give us all a good chance of getting crippled. Do you know, I like the idea of this little experiment. I like it very much. All you've got to do is open that front door and walk out. If we're wrong and you aren't their boy, they'll shoot as soon as you come out, at your legs. But if you are their own little stoolie, they won't shoot at all. They'll let you get across the street before they grab you. It's an even chance.'

The blond boy seemed incapable of movement. Another moment, Susan thought, and he'll be down on his knees.

'Off you go,' said the big man genially. 'Find the answer for us. Put us out of our misery. Move.'

The boy gave a last despairing look, turned and shambled out into the hall. They could hear the squeak of the rubber soles on the tiles of the hallway. Apart from this there was no sound at all, inside or outside the house.

The rattle of the chain being lifted. A click as the latch was turned.

The big man had moved back to the window. Susan said, very softly, 'If they *don't* shoot him—'

The big man seemed to be enjoying the situation. He said, 'If they don't shoot, then I shall. Not really an even chance. More a two way winner.' He was at the side window, which gave directly onto the porch and the front path. He eased it open a few inches and slid the muzzle of his gun over the sill.

As he did so, the front door came open and Blondie stumbled out. Before he got to the gate the shooting started. The bullets whipped across the small patch of garden and Blondie fell forward, screaming. The big man turned back into the room. He was much too late. Whilst his attention was on the scene outside, Susan had taken one step backwards to the mantelpiece, lifted the wilting chrysanthemums with her left hand and with her right hand eased out the .38 revolver which stood ready in the vase. It was now pointed at the big man. As his own hand came up, she pulled the trigger. The heavy bullet hit him square in the chest. He went down onto his knees, dropping his own gun, which slid away under the window seat. He had no eyes for it. He put both hands on the floor in front of him and tried to get up. The effort was too much. He stayed, crouched, his arms now wrapped round his chest as if he were holding himself together.

He said, 'I knew you were the sort of girl who'd pull the trigger. I told you so, didn't I?'

Susan nodded. She said, 'Yes, you told me.'

'Tell me something. I'd like to know. Did that kid give us away?'

'No. You gave yourself away. There was a six man team watching your every moment. They worked out your plan from your own moves. Incidentally, they spotted Blondie making that telephone call. It probably was to his girl.'

'I see.' The idea that he and not Blondie had been the traitor seemed to amuse him. He started to laugh, but stopped as the blood filled his lungs. When he was able to speak again he said, 'Tell me something else, before they get here.'

They had both heard the kitchen door go down. The police were coming in from the back of the house.

'I'd like to know your name.'

'It's Susan.'

'But not Susan Laybourne.'

'No. Susan Courtauld.'

'Courtauld. The name means something. I'm sure I heard it somewhere.'

The police were in the room by this time. Superintendent Collinson, who was leading them, said, 'We've sent for an ambulance.'

The big man took no notice of him. 'Courtauld,' he said. 'Now where did I hear that name?'

He was still puzzling over it when he died in the ambulance on the way to the hospital.

Michael Z. Lewin

THE RELUCTANT DETECTIVE

It started as a tax fiddle. Well, paint on a little semantic gloss: call it a tax avoidance structurisation. Uncle Edward would have preferred that, I think.

It was Uncle Edward who was responsible for my coming to England in the first place. I am American by birth and by upbringing. So was he, but some time in his relative youth he moved over here – I don't know what brought him – and he stayed. That was a long time ago, his moving. Before I was born. I'm twenty-six now. And I never actually met him, though I wrote to him often. Not letters exactly, because what we did was play postal chess. We did that over a period of more than ten years, so while I didn't know him at all, I felt I knew him fairly well. You get a sense of people by their chess games. Look at Anatoly Karpov's style on the board and you'll see a map of his face. No expression in either.

But that's by the by. I was Uncle Edward's only child-age relative – he never had kids of his own – and from the time I was born he kept in contact. He was quite close to his sister – my mother – and I always got a present on my birthday and at Christmas. It added a certain cosmopolitan touch to these occasions. And then he wrote direct to me when he heard from Mom that I had begun to play with the chess set he sent. We took it from there, playing by post till he died. Even during my years in college we kept it up. And afterwards too, when I was realising I didn't want to be a lawyer, no matter what Dad said about it being useful to fall back on even if I didn't know what I *really* wanted to do.

When Uncle Edward died I was sad. He was one of my few fixed points, a focus for a little contemplative time no matter where I was or what a shambles I was making of the rest of my life.

When I learned that Uncle Edward had provided for me in his will, I was astonished.

What I inherited was a house over here. Also a small income to be sent to me every month from the States. Just about enough to live on.

At first I didn't know what to do. Sell the house, or what. But when I thought about it, it occurred to me that if I thought I could tell about Uncle Edward from our chess games, maybe he could tell about me. Perhaps he was suggesting that it would be good for me to live in England for a while. I'm sure he knew from Mom that I was kind of at loose ends anyway because they wrote to each other. Actual letters, I mean. She only ever quoted to me from one once. When I asked her why Uncle Edward lived in England. She said he had written, *Britain is the closest thing there is left to a civilised English-speaking country.* 'He was never very good at languages,' she said after. The more I thought about it the better an idea it seemed. So I decided to give it a try, and over I came.

The tax fidd . . . tax avoidance structurisation didn't come up till I had been here a year or so. In fact, it was Dawn's idea, so in a way everything that's happened is down to her.

Dawn is the lady friend I've made. She is very civilised and if she is what Uncle Edward meant, I understand better why he spent his life here. It could happen to me, though that's not something I think about a lot.

Dawn agreed to move in after I'd been here about six months. We live in my house, and on my income. It gives us a lot of time to enjoy life. And think about things. We're not quite what they call drop-outs back home, because we intend to get into careers when we're sure what we want to do. But if we have no need to rush a decision . . . well, we didn't make the rules.

I see I'm already talking as if I am staying forever. Well, there are worse fates.

And, it turns out, we've already done something along a career line, even if it was strictly by accident. That's what this story is about.

OK, get the picture. I come over here to my house and an income. After six months Dawn and I are friends enough to live together. After six months we realise that comfortable as my income is, maybe there are things it would be nice to do if there were a little more money around.

Get a car for one. Nothing flash, but some wheels to see some of the rest of the country with.

Have I told you where I am? It's a little town in Somerset called Frome. (They pronounce it to rhyme with broom, by the way.) And it is pretty enough and in a lovely part of the country. But there are other places to see. Yes, it was considering getting a car that set us thinking in the first place.

Or set Dawn thinking, actually. She is the one who cooked it all up.

The idea was this. If I set up in business, as a self-employed person I could save money in taxes by deducting a lot of what we spent as necessary commercial expenses. Part of the house as an office; proportion of rates and heat and repairs and insurance; even a salary to Dawn as my secretary. And all the costs of my business vehicle.

Dawn worked it all out, and there was no question, it would pay for the car. And maybe a little bit more as we went along.

Then the question was what kind of business to supposedly set up in. That was Dawn's idea too. Well, not all ideas are necessarily bright.

I set up as a private detective. See, in Britain you don't need a licence of any kind. And, I have to admit, we yielded to a certain pleasant absurdity attached to the notion. I mean, a private detective, in Frome!

As well, the chances of anybody coming to us for business

were, of course, nil.

Which was the idea. We didn't want the business to succeed, or, indeed, for there to be any work at all. What we wanted were the deductions. It was a tax fiddle. As I've mentioned.

So, I bought a notebook and pen, and a small sign to put on the front of the house. It gave my name and said under it *Private Inquiry Agent* which is what they call private detectives here.

And that was it.

No advertisements, no listing in the Yellow Pages.

And no business.

We bought a little yellow Mini. Life as planned. It worked like a charm.

For a while.

It was a Tuesday, I remember, because I was reading the basketball column in *The Guardian* – I try to keep up with some of my old interests from the USA – when the doorbell rang. It was about ten o'clock. I thought it might be the gas man. Dawn was out visiting her mother – she's got as many relatives here as I have none, so to speak. A lot is what I am saying.

At the door was a sallow faced little man – well, I suppose he was about average height, but I am awkwardly tall, about 6′ 5″, so I have a distorted perspective on people. He had a jacket and tie on and he looked unhappy.

I thought, not the gas man but maybe a local government official.

'Are you Mr Herring?' he asked.

'Yes.'

'May I talk to you?'

'What about?' I asked.

He looked momentarily at the sign on the house by the door. It's so small you can hardly see it even if you know it's there. 'Are you the Mr Herring who is a private inquiry agent?'

And I suddenly realised he had come on business. I was stunned. I began to shake, though I don't know if he noticed.

'Yes, yes, of course,' I said. 'Fredrick Herring. Do come in.'

I led him to the living-room. It wasn't much to look at. Not for a detective's office. It was just a living-room, and lived in at that.

I sat him down. I didn't know what to say. But he made the running.

'My name is Goodrich,' he said.

'Hi.'

'I don't know whether I should even be here.'

'It's not a step to take lightly,' I said.

'I'm not,' he said. 'I'm not.'

'Oh.'

'I am a solicitor with Malley, Holmes and Asquith, but I need someone to make some inquiries for me on a private matter.'

'I see.'

'Well, you do that kind of thing, don't you?'

He looked at me. There was something devious in his eyes. And I had a sudden shock of suspicion.

You see, Dawn and I had talked about what to do if someone did actually come to us for work. We would just say that we were too busy to take the case on. But there was something about this man. The same thing that made me think he might be a council official. I got this idea that he was from one of the tax offices and that he was checking up on us.

It's just that on all these tax forms we'd been sending in we always had expenses listed, but never any income. It looked funny, of course. But economic times are hard and we assumed our amounts were so small, relatively, that nobody would notice.

But when you think you are being checked on, you suddenly feel the cold draught of accusation, prosecution.

'Of course,' I said.

Dawn was not pleased when she returned to the house and found that I had taken a case. But I explained my worries and she accepted the situation as a fact.

'It's about his brother-in-law, a guy named Chipperworth, who is a crook,' I said.

'Chipperworth . . .' Dawn said. She was thinking. She's lived in Frome all her life and knows a lot of people.

'He has a company that manufactures beds, up on the trading estate. The brand name is Rest Easy.'

'Ah.'

'You know it?'

'Rest Easy, yes.'

'And this man Goodrich says that Chipperworth set fire to a warehouse next to his factory up there and collected the insurance for it.'

'I read about the fire,' Dawn said. 'But not that it was on purpose. How does Goodrich know?'

'He says Chipperworth was bragging yesterday that he had just collected a cheque for over three hundred thousand pounds and it was for beds he wasn't going to be able to sell.'

'Good heavens,' Dawn said. 'But why doesn't Goodrich go to the police?'

'Because that's not what he's trying to sort out.'

'Oh.'

'What he's worried about is his sister. That Chipperworth is a crook, and that he's dangerous. He wants his sister to divorce Chipperworth.'

Dawn cocked her head.

'But his sister doesn't believe the stuff about the insurance fraud.'

'What are *we* supposed to do about that?'

'Goodrich wants us to prove Chipperworth has a woman on the side. If we can do that then the sister will divorce him and will be safe. Goodrich is sure that his sister will get a divorce in the end anyway, but if he precipitates it at least she'll be well off financially. If he waits till Chipperworth's activities catch up with him then it might ruin the sister too.'

'Oh,' Dawn said.

'I agreed to try.'

She nodded. Then she looked at me.

And I looked at her.

We were thinking the same thing.

I said, 'What the hell do we do now?'

Well, we had to go through the motions. The first motion was to find Chipperworth and identify him.

That wasn't hard. Mr Goodrich had given me a photograph and we decided to wait outside Rest Easy Beds toward the end of the work day. Rest Easy was not a big company. We counted about twenty people coming out after five-thirty. Chipperworth was the last and got into a B registered Sierra.

'OK,' Dawn said. 'There he is. What do we do now?'

'Drive along after him, I guess,' I said.

So we did. He went straight to a house on the Prowtings Estate. He pulled the car into the driveway. Got out. Went to the front door. Was met by a woman at 5.48 p.m. Then Chipperworth went into the house and closed the door.

That would have wrapped the case up if the woman hadn't been his wife.

Dawn and I sat.

'At least we know the registration number of his car now,' I said after ten minutes.

But we were both sinking fast.

After half an hour Dawn said, 'This is no good. What are we going to do, sit out here all night without any food or anything?'

And after some consideration of the situation, we decided to get fish and chips from Pangs. Even detectives have to eat.

When we got back, Chipperworth's car was gone.

Solicitor Goodrich rang up at nine the next morning. He seemed annoyed that I didn't have anything to report.

I explained that progress is not always rapid, that we'd had less than a day on the job.

But Goodrich knew that Chipperworth had been out the previous night. He'd called his sister and she told him.

'If you want to do the surveillance yourself,' I said, 'please say so. Otherwise, leave it to us.'

He took a breath, then apologised – rather unconvincingly I thought – and we hung up.

I told Dawn about the call.

'If we don't sort this out quickly,' she said, 'it's going to mess up our lives for weeks.'

'I know.'

'I'm going to see a couple of my cousins.'

I looked puzzled.

'Nigel is a telephone engineer,' she said. 'He's a nut case and would probably be willing to work out a way to tap the Chipperworths' telephone. And Paul works in the photographic section at Valets.' Valets was one of the local printing firms. 'He's a camera buff. He'll lend us a camera with a telephoto lens.'

'Right,' I said.

'We may have to borrow another car too, so we can cover Chipperworth the whole day. If it goes on for long we'll have to do shifts. I ought to be able to use Adele's Reliant. You remember Adele?'

'No.'

'She's the small one with the big –'

'I remember now,' I said.

Biggest feet I'd ever seen on a woman.

'I just wish I knew someone who could lend us a two-way radio.'

'There's your Uncle Mike,' I said.

'So there is,' she said. Then made a face. 'But he pinches and pokes whenever I get close enough and what he'd want for doing me a favour . . .'

'We'll get along without,' I said firmly.

In the end it only took a day.

It was the afternoon of my first shift. I was rigged up with a thermos, sandwiches and a radio. Even a specimen jar – from

Dawn's friend Elaine, the nurse – in case time was short and need was great.

When Dawn and I get down to it, we're impressive.

I took the afternoon shift because Dawn had to see her Auntie Wendy who was having troubles with a neighbour's boy picking on her son Edgar.

The camera was one of those instant print jobs. We'd talked it over with Paul and he figured that would be best. No time waiting for the film to come back from the developers. 'And,' he said, 'considering what kind of pictures you may get, a commercial firm might not print them.' Does a great leer, does Paul.

He also gave us a foot-long lens for the thing. 'It'll put you in their pockets,' he said. 'If they're wearing pockets.'

Cousin Nigel jumped at the chance to plant a tape recorder up a telephone pole to tap the Chipperworths' home phone. He volunteered to do the company phone too. Well, you don't turn down offers like that.

It's always struck me that all of Dawn's family are just that little bit shady. I offer it as an observation, not a complaint.

Anyway, after an hour's lunch at home, Chipperworth didn't go back to his office. He drove instead to Marston Road and pulled into the driveway of a detached brick house just beyond the end of speed restrictions. I drove past but parked immediately. I left the car and got the camera aimed and focused just in time to see Chipperworth open the door to the house with a key.

The picture came out a treat.

I stood there in the road looking at it. And wondering what to do next.

But Dawn and I had talked it through. First I made a note of the time, date and location on the back of the photograph. Then I set about trying to find out who lived in the house.

I went next door and rang the bell and had a little luck.

A tiny old woman with big brown eyes answered it. I said, 'Excuse me. I have a registered letter for the people next door

103

but nobody answers when I ring.'

'That's because Mrs Elmitt has her fancy man in,' the old woman said. 'And she wouldn't want to be disturbed now, would she? Some of the things I've seen! And they don't even bother to draw the curtains.'

Old women can do pretty good leers too, when they try.

Dawn was pleased as punch with me. I was pretty pleased myself. It meant that the wretched case would soon be over and we could get back to life as usual. I resolved to try to arrange for my income to arrive from America as some kind of retainer so that it looked like proceeds of the business. Then we wouldn't have to worry about being inspected by the tax people. Worry is a terrible thing.

But just about the time that we were getting ready to be pleased with each other, Cousin Nigel showed up at the front door.

He punched me on the shoulder as he came in, and gave Dawn a big kiss. A hearty type, Nigel.

'I've got your first tape,' he said jovially. 'Went up to see if it needed changing and blow me if there hadn't been a lot of calls. Thought you would want to hear them sooner rather than later, so I put another cassette in the machine and brought this one right over. Got any beer while we listen to it?' He dropped into our most comfortable chair. 'Hey Dawnie, how about something to eat? Egg and chips? Hungry work, bugging telephones.'

The tape was a revelation.

Right off, the very first phone call had things like the man saying, 'Darling, I can't wait until I see you again.'

And the woman: 'I don't know whether I'll be able to bear not being with you all the time for very much longer.'

'It will be soon. We'll be together, forever. Somewhere nice. Away from your wretched husband.'

'I don't know what will become of me if our plan doesn't work.'

104

'It will work. We'll make it work.'

'Oh darling, I hope so.'

And on and on, that kind of mushy stuff. There were a lot of slobbering sounds too. I would have been embarrassed if I hadn't been so upset.

'Wow!' Nigel said. 'All that kissy-kissy, and before lunch. They must have it bad.'

Dawn said, 'Isn't that great! We've got all we need now, Freddie, don't you think?'

But I was not happy, not even close.

Because, unlike my two colleagues, I had recognised one of the voices. The man's. The conversation was not between Mr Chipperworth and Mrs Elmitt. The man on the telephone was our client, Mr Goodrich, and the object of his affection was, presumably, Mrs Chipperworth, his "sister".

We got rid of Nigel before we talked it out.

'I guess this means that our client was not being completely open and frank with us,' Dawn said.

There was no law that a client had to tell us the truth. But neither of us liked it.

'But what do we do?'

We had a long chat about it.

What we did was go the next morning to Dawn's Uncle Steve, who is a police sergeant. We asked him about the fire in the Rest Easy Beds warehouse.

'Always knew it was arson,' Uncle Steve said. 'But we couldn't prove who did it. The owner was the only possible beneficiary, but he had an airtight alibi. Not quite as good as being out to dinner with the Chief Superintendent, but he was at a function with the Mayor and he was at a table, in full sight, the whole evening.'

'I see,' Dawn said.

'I interviewed Chipperworth myself,' Uncle Steve said, 'and he was quite open about being delighted about the fire. Business wasn't very good and he was having trouble moving the stock that was destroyed. Personally, I don't think he *did* have anything to do with it. I've been at this job long enough to get a good sense of people and that's the way he came across.'

'I see,' Dawn said.

'But we never got so much as a whiff of any other suspect. Checked through all current and past employees for someone with a grievance. Sounded out all our informants in town for a word about anybody who might have been hired to do the deed or who heard anything about it. But we didn't get so much as a whisper. It's very unusual for us not to get some kind of lead if something's bent and we try that hard. In the end, it was written off to kids. There are so many around with nothing to do these days that we're getting all sorts of vandalism.'

'Thanks, Uncle Steve,' Dawn said.

'Helps you, does that?' he asked.

'I think so.'

'If you know anything about the case, you must tell us. You know that, don't you?'

'Yes, Uncle Steve.'

He looked at her and shook his head. Then he said to me, 'Young man, there is a look in her eye that I don't like. There's something tricky about all her people. You watch yourself.'

He was right, of course. Dawn was cooking something up, and it wasn't chips.

When we got home we sat down over a nice cup of tea. She hadn't said a word during the whole drive.

I couldn't bear it any longer. I said, 'All right. What *is* the significance of that funny look?'

'I've decided we're going to get Mrs Chipperworth that divorce our client wants after all.'

'We are?'

'It's what we were hired to do, isn't it?'

I called Solicitor Goodrich to tell him that we had had success in our investigation and did he want our report.

He did. He was with us within twenty minutes.

I explained what I had seen the previous afternoon. I gave him the photographs I had taken of Chipperworth entering Mrs Elmitt's house with a key and, later, adjusting his flies as he came out. I reported what the neighbour had told me.

'She is willing to testify to what she's seen in court, or to swear out a statement,' I said. 'But she would like some money for it.'

'I think that can be arranged,' Goodrich said.

A little ready cash might help the old woman get some curtains for her own windows.

Goodrich wrote out a cheque for our fee and expenses on the spot.

'Of course, if *we* have to testify,' I said, 'there will be an additional bill.'

'I don't think it will come to that,' Goodrich said.

After he left I rang Rest Easy Beds.

I explained to Mr Chipperworth that we wanted to come over to speak to him.

'What is it that is so urgent, Mr Herring?' he asked.

'We wanted to tell you about your wife's plans to sue you for divorce,' I said.

As soon as we arrived we were ushered into Chipperworth's office.

'But she's known about Madeleine for years,' he said when I explained what we'd been hired to do. 'It's an arrangement we have. She doesn't like *it*, you see. So Madeleine keeps me from making . . . demands.'

'She doesn't seem to mind the demands of her lover,' Dawn said.

'Her *what*?'

'Why don't you ask her about her telephone calls recently,' Dawn suggested. 'We have to be going now. Ta ta.'

We stopped at Nigel's and then we went on home.

We didn't have long to wait.

A few minutes after noon the bell rang. Before I could get to it, pounding started on the door. When I opened it I faced Solicitor Goodrich, in a fury. He swung fists at me.

For the most part being as tall as I am is an inconvenience. But at least I have long arms and could keep him out of reach. When he finished flailing, he started swearing. The rude language seemed particularly unseemly for a member of the legal profession. I would have been very embarrassed for Dawn if I hadn't heard as bad or worse from her family. But they are foul-mouthed in a friendly way. Goodrich was vicious.

Also defamatory. He claimed that we had sold information to Mr Chipperworth.

I was about to deny it when Dawn said, 'What if we did?'

'I'll have you for this,' Goodrich said. 'It's illegal. I can put you in gaol.'

'That's fine talk from somebody who set fire to a warehouse.'

Goodrich was suddenly still and attentive. 'What?'

'You're the arsonist responsible for the fire at Rest Easy Beds.'

'That's silly talk,' Goodrich said. But he wasn't laughing.

'The idea was that when Mr Chipperworth collected the insurance money Mrs Chipperworth would start divorce proceedings which would entitle her to claim half of it. With your help she could probably settle out of court and between the insurance cash and her share of the rest of the joint property, you and Mrs Chipperworth would have a nice little nest egg to run away on.'

'Prove it,' Goodrich said.

'Oh, I think it's a very clever plan,' Dawn said charmingly. 'I suppose you have an alibi for the night of the fire?'

'Why should I need one?'

'Well, if we went to the police . . .'

'Why the hell should you do that?' Goodrich burst out.

'Ah,' Dawn said. 'Now we're getting down to the serious questions.' She batted her eyelashes. 'We never actually gave our evidence to Mr Chipperworth, you know, and as long as Mrs Chipperworth has denied everything . . .'

'You want money, I suppose,' Goodrich said.

'Well, poor Freddie is terribly tall, and a bigger car would be so much easier for him to get in and out of.'

'All right,' Goodrich said. 'A car.'

'And there are so many little improvements that ought to be made on this house.'

'How about just getting to a bottom line figure.'

'I think thirty thousand would come in very handy, don't you Freddie?'

'Oh, very handy.'

'Thirty thousand!' Goodrich said.

'Yes,' Dawn said. 'See how reasonable we are!'

When the trial came along it was plastered all over the local papers. Frome is not so big a town that we get serious court cases involving local people every week.

Especially not cases involving solicitors and arson, not cases with a little titilation in them. Goodrich pleaded guilty, but the local reporter, Scoop Wall, tracked down Mrs Elmitt's neighbour who was photographed pointing to some of the uncurtained windows through which she had been forced to witness indescribable acts. Well, the descriptions didn't make the papers anyway.

Uncle Steve was not pleased at first when he heard what we had done.

Heard is the operative word because we had tape-recorded the entire conversation with Goodrich on equipment we borrowed from Cousin Nigel.

But Dawn explained. After all this time the only way Goodrich's arson would be proved was if he confessed to it. But the police couldn't have used the threat of exposing his relationship to Mrs Chipperworth the way we did because that would have transgressed legal niceties. 'So it was up to Freddie and me,' Dawn said.

Eventually Uncle Steve laughed.

'I warned you about her,' he said to me.

But it worked out all right in the end.

Except . . . Scoop Wall tracked down Dawn and me too.

We begged her not to put anything about us in the paper.

But she refused. We were key figures in bringing a dangerous solicitor to justice. It was news. And besides, Dawn has good legs and photographs well.

It's not that we weren't proud of what we – or let's be fair – what Dawn had done.

But it meant that the Fredrick Herring Private Inquiry Agency burst from its quiet and planned total obscurity into the glare of public attention.

We started getting calls. We started getting visitors. We started getting letters. Find this, look for that, unravel the other.

And it wasn't actually the attention which was the problem.

The problem was that we found we quite liked it. See, some of the cases we were offered were pretty interesting. Rather like chess problems . . . So, we decided, maybe one more. Or two.

James McClure

REMEMBER THAT JOKE, HARRY?

For just over a week now, Patrol Officer Harry T. Lomas had been working downtown San Diego under protest, and the continual round of the bus benches, the detoxification centre on Island Avenue, the bus benches, another lousy stinking drunk, the detox, was really getting to him. Getting to him so bad that he was using damn near a can a day of Julliet's Apple Blossom Air Sweetna on the rear seat of his unit. It was becoming the breath of life to him. He was hooked on it. Anything that didn't smell of apple blossom was a turn-off.

'Hey, what's the matter, Harry?' Debbie had asked in bed that morning. 'Somethin' I said was wrong? You wanna try a different position?'

Harry hadn't been able to tell her that she stank of a fresh clean young body.

And now, to add to his troubles, here was this dude lying in the trash at the back of Juicy Lucy's on F Street, pissing a pretty fountain of blood in the air. Or at least that's what it looked like, but Harry was working for his Emergency Medical Treatment badge, and knew the femoral artery had been slashed.

Three in the groin in three days.

It was close to an epidemic.

'I'm dyin' . . .' groaned the latest victim.

'Oh, OK,' said Harry. 'But before you do that, I'd kinda like a description.' Then he handed his flashlight to a

113

hovering pimp to hold while he got himself dirty. 'Who stuck ya, buddy?'

But the man only groaned louder as Harry dug in a thumb, trying to find the right pressure point. He missed it and blood drenched the front of his tan uniform. That was another thing about working downtown: Harry was getting through clean uniforms faster than a circus chimp through diapers.

'Who stuck ya?' Harry persisted. 'You want the mother to run free, huh?'

'Nobody,' the victim said between clenched teeth. 'There was *nobody*. Didn't see nothin' . . .'

Harry tugged at the guy's zipper. His pants were all bunched up and getting in the way of things. They were going to have to come off.

'You and you,' ordered Harry. 'Grab and pull.'

'Oh my, my, my!' wailed a black hooker when she saw the hacked-up mess between those skinny white thighs.

You didn't need a vested interest to feel a little upset by the sight. A crippled Indian on crutches took one look and fell on his ass, while a wino went bug-eyed and barfed straight back into his bottle.

'Cool it, will ya?' Harry said irritably. 'I gotta concentrate . . .'

This time his attempt to find the right pressure point seemed to work a little. The jet of blood lost height, dwindled right down and turned into a fat rosebud that wobbled and changed shape all the time, like in one of those movies where they show you a flower growing from seed to full bloom in under two minutes.

'That's hurtin', pig!' complained the victim. 'Fuck you, pig! What the fuck ya doin'?'

'Testin' your reflexes,' said Harry. 'You reflexed good.'

'I did?'

'How come a smart dude like you got taken in this alley? No place a man could hide, the light ain't bad, and –'

'I was lookin', man! Hey, I was lookin' all round and I didn't see no –'

'Nobody ever tell you, asshole, you need eye-glasses?'

'Shit, I don't need no eye-glasses!' The victim arched up, grimaced in agony, and flopped back again. Then he began to speak more sincerely, like he'd realised he was nearing his Maker. 'Listen, officer, the only way I can figure it, he got me from behind.'

'He snuck up over all this trash? How come you didn't hear anythin'?'

'Heard nothin'.'

'Hear anythin' now?'

The paramedics had their siren yelping as they approached along Broadway. A faint sound, growing louder.

'An ambulance?' said the victim.

'Terrific. You can hear good, you can see good. But you didn't hear or see the mother that jumped ya by the trash cans. What was he – invisible?'

'That's right,' said the victim, going slack. 'He was fuckin' invisible.'

The paramedics came up the alley at the run, crunching over the trash in their combat boots, toting a whole heap of lifesaving equipment. They gave Harry a superior kind of smile, and reached for their holstered stethoscopes.

'Take it easy, guys,' said Harry. 'I've been doin' a great job here. There's nothing to listen to.'

The sergeant in charge of Homicide Team Five was a brisk, very businesslike redhead with boobs small enough not to get in the way of her determination to be treated strictly on her merits as an investigator. The only problem being that right now, after three killings in a row, and no suspect in sight, her merits didn't amount to much either.

'Oh, Jesus, Harry,' she sighed, 'is that all you can come up with? It's been the same each goddam time. The first two said they'd not seen anythin' either before he hit 'em. Just *pow* . . .'

115

'Beats me,' agreed Harry. 'He got it by those trash cans, but they sure aren't big enough for a guy to hide behind, and—'

'What was his reason for bein' in this alley?'

'I guess,' said Harry, savouring the humour of what he was about to add, 'the dude had in mind taking himself a short cut.'

Sergeant Brunowski smiled, only a little. 'You got some ID on him? First thing we'll do is run a check, see if he connects up with the first two.'

'Robert Ajax Arno,' said Harry. 'Don't worry, he'll connect. They all connect on F Street. I've seen him here a coupla times, talkin' to a fat Chicano.'

'I mean connect in some special way. Shit, this is your beat! Is that the best you can do for me?'

Harry bristled. 'The hell this pile o' crud's my beat! My beat's Balboa Park, right? I'm just fillin' in for J.P. —'

'Harry, we all know how you feel, sugar,' said Brunowski, and there was no empathy in her voice, none. 'But while you're assigned to downtown, you'd better show with some ideas – OK?'

He looked up and down the alley. It sure was a place he'd never want to walk through out of uniform. On nights when the fog was bad, it could scare you half to death just to peer into it.

'Hey, I gotta idea!' he said. 'To do with fog.'

'Fog? In *July*?'

'No, lemme explain. These are all sex killings, right?'

'Sex-related.'

'Sure, but some kinda sex motive is involved. I read about that Jack the Ripper guy one time, and these killin's match up pretty well in terms of target area.'

'You're not always easy to follow, Harry. The victims were all hookers, all women . . .'

'Uh-huh, and these victims have all been men – get it? The switch-around? Sort of Jill the Ripper?'

Brunowski nodded. 'It's got possibilities.'

'Like you agree a chick could . . .'

'Sure, I've felt that way about a guy a few times myself,' said Brunowski, introducing a chill to Harry's jockey shorts. 'OK, I'll get the team workin' on that angle, see if we can't come up with some female they could've given a bad time to or somethin'. Thanks, kid.'

'It was nothin',' said Harry, modestly.

'No, it wasn't a lot,' said Brunowski. 'Now instead of an invisible man, we're out lookin' for an invisible woman. I ask myself, is this really progress?'

Next day, Harry began his shift determined to stay clean. He became blind to blind drunks, deaf to deafening obscenities, and plain indifferent to the public's provocative behaviour in general. He could not ignore his radio, however, and when directed to cover a colleague answering a four-fifteen at the Viceroy Hotel on Third, he reacted like any good cop and burned rubber getting there.

The Viceroy was a roach farm. Three dollars a night, and in a righteous world they'd have given you your money back in the morning, just for having survived it that long. Things that'd crawled out from under rocks used the Viceroy, and when they became too drunk or too doped to go out and mug somebody, rape somebody, they just went into the room next to their own and did it there. The place also had a handful of semi-permanent residents too crazy or too weird or too freakish to care whether this happened to them. A fat lady so fat she bent bath tubs, a guy with a trunk who made the Elephant Man look as cuddly as Dumbo; a hulk in Room 512 that crooned away to itself in a deep husky voice, interminably. In short, the Viceroy wasn't the kind of hotel Harry had in mind for his wedding night with Debbie, even if this meant they were going to have to save some.

Art was standing beside his unit outside the front entrance. 'Hi, Harry,' he said, 'Room Four-one-eight. Clerk says there's been glass breakin' and a guy yellin' in there.'

117

'Couldn't it be that he just likes yellin' and breakin' glass?'

'Uh-huh, but maybe we ought to check with him.'

Together, they entered the hotel lobby. Along the stained walls stood snack machines, three pay phones, and a wire rack in which guests were instructed to place their empty bottles. The hotel clerk was over on the left, behind a cage of iron bars and heavy-gauge wire mesh. He didn't even bother to look up as they stepped into the elevator.

It had to be the scariest elevator in the whole of San Diego. There were no proper doors and it had no buttons to press, just a lever sticking out of a dented metal box. To go up, you pulled the lever; to go down, you pushed it; to stop, you tried to position it dead-centre or it'd start acting like a Yo-yo.

'You got the training,' Harry said to Art, who'd flown choppers in Vietnam. 'You do it.' The lever looked unpleasantly sticky.

But the elevator had to think first. It just sat there a while. Then it began to rise, gathering momentum as though determined this time to go soaring up, break clear through the roof of the Viceroy, and go someplace where people wouldn't spit and piss in it.

Art had to move fast. 'Fourth,' he said, bringing the elevator to a knee-sagging halt. 'Don't fall on your ass over Franklin J.'

But Franklin J. Abercrombie, a twenty-six-inch high midget who always rushed to see who was coming out of the elevator, wasn't around for once. Instead, there was this wild-eyed Mexican momma with a broken bottle in her fist.

'Hold it right there, lady!' warned Harry, shouting because his Spanish was terrible and he wasn't speaking Spanish anyway. 'DROP IT, lady!'

Art found a quicker way round the language barrier: he hit her wrist with his night-stick.

The bottle shattered on the floor, she cut her foot and started hollering, which brought help from every doorway down the hall. It wasn't until Harry and Art had drawn their handguns, and things had quietened down a little, that they learned from a

118

skinny guy in an undershirt it'd been the Mexican momma who had called them to the Viceroy. She had been trying to show them the bottle she'd been threatened with.

'Oh, OK,' said Art. 'Where's the guy who tried to attack her?'

'She says the dude split ten minutes back. What took you so long?'

Art's broad shoulders slumped. 'Ten minutes? What kinda description she got?'

Meanwhile an old lush in a filthy housecoat said to Harry, 'You wanna put somebody in jail? You put my husband in jail, the sonavabitch. Don't you ever let him out again!'

'How come?' said Harry, with his attention on the Mexican momma, trying to read her gestures.

'You know what he did?' slurred the lush. 'What that no-good, lyin' sonavabitch said? Said he knew a place he could get me a luxury casket for two hundred bucks outa the funeral money I got stashed. *Real* luxury, know what I mean? With the silver fittin's and the satin and the lacey pillow? Worth a grand retail, he said, but Bobby Arno'd let him have it for –'

'You ready to roll, Harry?' Art cut in. 'We're lookin' for a male Caucasian, around six-one and one-eighty pounds.'

'Sure, I'm ready.'

'Hey, officer, I'm tellin' you my story! But when the sonavabitch comes back, he ain't got no casket – and he ain't got no money. "Okay, where's the two hundred?" I ask him. First, he says –'

'Your name is, ma'am?' interrupted Harry.

'Mrs Wilma Johnson.'

'You wanna press charges, Mrs Johnson, you go down the station on Market – tell the nice officer there, OK? Me and my partner, we're in a kinda hurry right now.'

Harry and Art turned back toward the elevator and almost tripped over Franklin J. Abercrombie, standing there in his dinkie little bathrobe, towelling his hair.

'Hi, officers!'

119

'Hi, Franklin J.,' said Harry. 'How're ya doin'?'

'Pretty good,' said the midget, winking. 'Always feel pretty good after a shower, so long as I don't slip down the plughole!' His laugh was a falsetto cackle. 'See you round.'

'Sure,' grunted Harry, 'we'll be back.'

That was something which could always be safely said about the Viceroy.

Art moved the lever cautiously and the elevator began a jerky descent. 'Goddamn,' he said, 'I've finally figured out why Franklin J. lives in this fleabag. Remember that joke, Harry? There's this guy who lives on the thirtieth floor of an apartment building. Every morning, when he goes to work, he rides the elevator down to street level. Every night, when he comes back from the office, he takes the elevator up to the eighteenth, then uses the stairs for the rest of the way. Now why does he do that, for Chrissakes? It isn't for the exercise.'

Harry snapped his fingers. 'Hey, go back up!' he ordered.

'What'd you leave behind this time?'

'That Ma Johnson, she said something about "Bobby Arno" – could be the same Robert Ajax Arno that bought his lunch in the alley last night.'

'And so?'

'Sounded like he could've taken her old man for two hundred bucks.'

'Big deal.'

'Hey, just do like I say, OK?'

The elevator stopped at the lobby. 'It's all yours, pal,' said Art, stepping out. 'Code Seven at the Green Fly?'

'This is no time to be thinking of food,' said Harry.

Mrs Wilma Johnson sat on a sagging bed surrounded by empty white port bottles and heckled by a mean-eyed green parrot in a cage with more bends in its bars than a liquor store's back window.

'You know how it is,' she was saying. 'You don't put somethin' by, and the city dumps you down some hole someplace in a splintery ol' box.'

'Uh-huh,' said Harry. 'Maybe you haven't been able to live good, but you're sure gonna die good! My mom was the same way.'

'She was?'

'So what happened?'

'*Asshole!*' shrieked the parrot.

'That's right, my asshole of a husband, so called, takes my two hundred and it's *three goddamn days* before he comes by again, fulla crap that he'd been in Community with a busted head after bein' beaten on and robbed. Said he'd had am-somethin', couldn't remember nothin'.'

'Nothin' at all?'

'Oh sure, he'd tried to get me the casket, he said. Had gone to this address on Imperial that Bobby Arno'd given him, only some chick there had said it'd been sold the same morning.'

'You believed that?'

'I beat on him a little, and he wrote out the address – here, take a look for yourself – and said I should go, check it out for myself. Can you imagine? A lady like me, wantin' to be seen in that kinda neighbourhood?'

Harry memorised the address. 'And you're sure it was Bobby Arno who tried to sell him the casket? Bobby Arno as in Robert Ajax Arno?'

'As in county morgue,' said Mrs Johnson, nipping at a fifth of cheap rye. 'Bastid.'

'*Bastid! Bastid! Bastid!*' chanted the parrot, adding a high cackle.

'Uh-huh, and Mr Johnson? Any idea where we can contact him?'

'County morgue too, I hope,' said Mrs Johnson.

So Harry took his unit round to the address on Imperial, and found it was a small house with adobe walls and Spanish tiles, half-smothered in bougainvillea. The path up from the gate was a mess of weeds, which deadened the sound of his approach, and before he knocked at the front door, he took a peep through the nearest window. There was a foxy little lady stuffing clothes into a cheap drug-store suitcase with a red plaid top. She was going at it as though there were three feet left between the Titanic and the iceberg.

He rang the doorbell and heard her gasp. 'Police department!' he called out.

She came to the window to check him first, also took a look at his unit, then opened the front door a crack.

'What you doin' here?' she asked, her voice unnecessarily low.

'Lady, I was just cruisin' by, and I seen a shadowy shape runnin' from your porch,' Harry lied effortlessly.

'You *what*?' she said, grabbing him by the arm and pulling him inside before slamming the door. 'You gotta help me, officer!'

'Harry T. Lomas,' said Harry. 'And yours?'

'Juniper Rodak.'

Like her name, she started out pretty and ended up not too alluring. The face was nice, and so were the pair of soft round globes inside her black blouse, worn over a red skirt flouncy enough for the flamenco. But those big blue eyes had dilated pupils, there were needle bruises in the crooks of her elbows, and her body smelled a lot more like mushroom than apple blossom.

'Juniper Rodak?' Harry repeated after her, certain he'd seen "Rodak" typed on a green report form only recently. 'Hey, weren't you Leroy Master's chick – the dude who got it in the groin Tuesday?'

She nodded. Then it all came out in a rush. Leroy had got his Tuesday, Clarence 'The Hump' Bernstein had been unhung Wednesday, and she'd just got to hear about Bobby Arno's demise in the alley last night, which had left her finally scared mindless.

'Take me to jail,' she begged, tightening her grip on his arm. 'Bust me! I'm not picky what for, just get me the hell outa here

122

somewhere that's safe!'

'You knew all three guys?' he asked. 'How come?'

'Leroy.'

'Uh-huh?'

'He had this casket, asked me if I could keep it here at my place. The Hump and Bobby helped him bring it round, then all these people kept comin' and comin', wantin' to buy it.'

'Where'd Leroy get it from, Juniper?'

'Jesus Christ, how should I know! You think I used to ask him that kinda question? You must be crazy!'

Harry freed his arm from her grasp. 'Then I guess you better handle this on your own, lady. I thought I might just get your co-operation.'

'You *got* my co-operation!' she said desperately, grabbing for the hem of her skirt.'You got anythin' you want, officer – right here on the hall floor if you like! Just get me the hell outa here!'

'But what makes you so scared, Juniper? Tell me that.'

'You don't see a connection?' she replied. 'These three guys were all in on the casket caper, all three guys have been – I mean, I could be the *fourth*, right?'

'So you know of nobody else involved?'

She frowned a tiny frown. 'Maybe I heard them say somethin' about another chick bein' in on it, somebody they'd kinda used for somethin'. Never heard her name, though.'

'Harry,' said Brunowski, 'you're a boy genius.'

'It was nothin',' he said.

'No, it wasn't much,' she agreed, getting into the front seat of his unit with him, 'you were handed it practically on a plate.'

'But we gotta pattern now, Sarge.'

'Sure, we got a pattern! But what sort of sense does it make? It was a whole lot easier when we thought these killings had to be sex-related. But *casket*-related, f'Chrissake?'

Harry shrugged. 'Kinda unusual, I guess,' he conceded. 'Maybe if we knew where the casket had come from, that'd be a help.'

'Don't be such an asshole!' snapped Brunowski. 'There's only one place a casket could come from – a funeral home.'

'Or funeral home supplier.'

'Where does that get us? There is no way I'm buying the idea some mortician's so sore about havin' one of his caskets ripped off that he's goin' round –'

'Me neither,' said Harry. 'But you gotta start somewhere.'

'Motive, Harry, that's where it's at. Find the *motive*. Did Rodak get a look in this casket? Was there somethin' hidden in it?'

'I thought of that, Sarge. She said it looked totally legit, a little on the extra large side. Guy who bought it was an old-timer in tennis shoes.'

'How much did he pay?'

'Juniper can't tell us that. All she knew was that Leroy said a three-way split would still bring him some fat.'

'A three-way split?'

'Uh-huh.'

'Then that's it!' said Brunowski, showing her excitement by giving Harry a painful punch on the shoulder. 'How come they were splitting it three ways when there were four of them in it? They double-crossed her!'

'Juniper'd never –'

'No, the other female she didn't know the name of. She must've been as mad as a snake at 'em!'

'Mad enough to give it to them in the crotch?' said Harry, and his voice sounded awful doubtful.

'Sure, they'd fucked her around, right? It would be kinda symbolical.'

'Sarge, we're not talkin' big money here,' Harry reminded her. 'A fourth share in around two hundred –'

'The bitch is a doper, right? She needs every buck she can lay hands on. Now you know as well as I do that there's nothing meaner than a mainliner who gets double-crossed out of a fix by –'

'The dope makes her invisible?' objected Harry. 'What is she shootin' up – Vanishing Juice?'

'Ah,' said Brunowski, 'I'd not forgotten. It wasn't these three males didn't see her; it was they didn't want to cop out they'd been caught flat-footed by a female.'

'Jesus, that's pretty damn weak, Sarge.'

'Is that right?' said Brunowski, starting to get out of the unit. 'You've forgotten your idea yesterday that the perpetrator could be a woman?'

'No, but –'

'Then let me tell you somethin', Harry,' she said. 'Do you think you've been the only one working on this case? My team is just through interviewing everyone they could find who was near the alley at the time of the stabbing. Three of 'em – *three* witnesses, Harry – have all come up with the same thing. They say they heard a female laffin' her ass off back there in the alley, just before you rolled up and started complaining about getting your uniform dirty.'

'They did?'

'And they're ready to swear to it. "A high, girlish laugh", quote, unquote. Where's Rodak?'

'Down at the detox for safekeeping. I heard you up here and so I just –'

'Hmmm, I've got a coupla good questions for her,' interrupted Brunowski.

'What about me, Sarge?'

'You're Patrol, so patrol, Harry,' said Brunowski, stepping out. Then she wrinkled her nose and added, 'Anybody ever tell you your unit smelled like a goddamn orchard?'

Harry stayed right where his unit was parked. Brunowski, he felt convinced, had allowed a little too much of her women's liberation thing to creep into her interpretation of the facts. Neither was he happy about having been called an asshole. It really rankled.

Rankled so much that he got on the radio and asked for a computer search. He wanted to know if there had been a report of a casket having been stolen from a funeral home or other likely source. No insurance company was going to pay out unless a report had been made.

'Negative,' said the despatcher at Communications.

Then the cat would have to be skinned some other way. Maybe Pa Johnson had known more about the casket he'd set out to buy than he'd told his ever-lovin' wife Wilma and the parrot. From the sound of things, she hadn't given him much time to talk at all.

Harry found Johnson holed up in a bar ten blocks from the Viceroy, licking his wounds over a pitcher of cold beer. He had so many yards of white bandage around his head it was like talking to a snowman. He had coal-black eyes, teeth missing in the front, and a long raw nose like a carrot.

'How d'ya know where I was?' said Johnson, startled.

'Vice Squad,' replied Harry, being prepared to trade a little honesty for a lot of honesty in return. 'By this time of night, they've checked out most bars south of Broadway. You were, er, kinda easy for them to remember.'

Johnson started to get up. 'Shit,' he said, 'if Wilma –'

'Take it easy, be cool,' said Harry, poking him back into his seat with the tip of his night-stick. 'She's so juiced up she probably can't make it to the bathroom right now, never mind ten blocks. I want to ask you about that mighty fine casket.'

'Fuck the casket!' said Johnson.

'And the two hundred dollars?'

'So that's it,' murmured Johnson, sighing and slumping. 'The bitch. Didn't I tell her what happened?'

'Yeah, and Community Hospital told *me*,' said Harry, 'that you were never near the place. Are you goin' to level?'

'I never did steal that two hundred!'

'Then let's hear what did happen,' suggested Harry, taking the seat opposite him.

Johnson leaned forward, an old con man's trick to set up a rapport. 'You gotta try and picture how I felt, officer,' he said. 'When I first told Wilma about the casket, a light came on in her eyes. That's right, she just lit up! She was so goddamm happy! How could I go back there to the Viceroy and say some other guy'd gotten in ahead of me? So I had this great idea, got to hear where there was this little poker game goin', and I was aimin' to –'

'OK, OK,' said Harry, who'd definitely heard this one before, 'don't break my heart, pal, just tell me about the dude who gave you the address on Imperial.'

'Just some guy I'd seen around.'

'Bobby Arno?'

Johnson flinched. 'Yeah, Bobby,' he mumbled.

'He told you it was big and pretty?'

'Luxury model, he said. Big enough for a stiff six-six.'

'What else? That it'd been boosted?'

'Er, he kinda laughed a lot.'

'Uh-huh?'

'He's gone now, poor sucker, so what the hell, I'll tell you, officer. He gave me the idea the way they'd got it was – well, humorous, I'd guess you'd call it.'

'From a funeral home?'

'Hell, no. It was some freaky guy who had it stashed away for his own use some day. Been seen by a cleaner.'

'What freaky guy?'

'They never said. Swore there'd be no trouble. The guy wouldn't have wanted anybody to know he'd had it.'

'That's what interests me,' said Harry, finding this all a little hard to swallow. 'Who would want to have a casket hangin' 'round ahead of time?'

Johnson shrugged. 'Some dude who thinks a lot of dyin'?'

'But why do that?'

'Jesus, how da fuck should I know? Because he's got cancer? Been told he's got six months to go? Figure it out yourself, will ya? I'm not on the pay roll of the department!'

'But do you know anybody answerin' that description?'

'Can't say I do,' replied Johnson, taking a sip of his beer with some difficulty through the gap in his bandages. 'There's that thin guy, same floor as me at the Viceroy. I heard tell that he's pretty sick.'

Harry had grown to like the old bastard a lot less in the short time he'd known him, but suddenly had to resist an impulse to hug Johnson outright. 'Height around six-four, six-five!' he said. 'You know his name?'

'Rikki Sullivan, goes round in an undershirt and – hey, *wait* a minute!'

But Harry was gone.

He knew he was playing a long shot. A very long shot. But the feeling that went with it was good.

Then Brunowski came through on his handie-talkie radio just as Harry was about to step into the elevator at the Viceroy. 'I just wanted to tell you, boy genius,' she said, 'how much I admire you.'

'Is that right, Sarge?' he said cautiously.

'You want to know why, Harry? Because I'm down here at the detox and you'll never guess who Patrol just brought in. The mystery chick.'

'The one who worked the casket caper with the three guys?'

'Affirmative. She's got blood all over her – says she got busted on the nose by some other drunk on Broadway, but I'm hoping she'll see reason pretty soon. She doesn't want to talk to me right now.'

'But how did you get an ID on her?'

'Juniper Rodak recognised her as a female Leroy Masters was whisperin' to at a party a few weeks ago. Leroy then told Bobby Arno he'd fixed her up to lay some guy. If you haven't guessed she's a hooker – name of Wanda la Douche.'

'Oh boy, another one with imagination,' he said.

'Well, that's about it, Harry,' said Brunowski, 'just thought you'd like to know. One other thing: her goddamn arms are full of holes – she's mainlining.'

Harry hitched the handie-talkie to his gunbelt and gave a long sigh. It no longer seemed worth risking the elevator up to the fourth floor. From the sound of it, Homicide Team Five had things sewn up down there at the detox. Then on impulse, like a nickel gambler passing a fruit machine, he made a grab for the elevator lever.

'What the hell,' said Harry.

Things started to go wrong. He stepped out of the elevator and almost fell over Franklin J. Abercrombie. 'F'Chrissakes, Franklin, will ya stop gettin' under my fuckin' feet, OK?'

'I'm sorry, really sorry,' said the midget, looking hurt.

'Sullivan's room – what number?'

'Down the end, officer, beside the Johnsons'. Did he call you? Is he – ?'

'Get lost,' growled Harry.

Next came the sinking feeling in the pit of his stomach when Sullivan opened his door. One glance was enough to see that there'd never have been enough space in that crowded little room in which to accommodate a six-foot-six casket. The place was almost shoulder-deep in old magazines and newspapers.

Sullivan, thin and yellow-skinned in his undershirt, said, 'Come right in, officer – been expectin' you.'

Harry went into the room. 'You have?' he said.

'The police, always got to write everything down,' said Sullivan. 'You want me to tell you about the guy with the bottle?'

'Oh, that? No, not right now, I'm workin' on a different investigation.'

'And I can help?'

'Er, it was just somethin' about a casket, but –'

'The casket the Johnsons wanted to buy that was going so cheap?'

'How did you know that?'

'These walls aren't up to much, officer. It's often hard for a man *not* to know his neighbour's business, specially when voices get raised.'

'Well, what can you tell me about it?'

'That he went to a certain address on Imperial and he didn't get it.'

'Oh, terrific. You mean that's *all* you know?'

'Right.'

Harry looked round at the piles of papers and magazines. 'You doin' some kinda research, maybe?' he asked, having noted that Sullivan spoke educated.

The man gave a slight smile, like an Egyptian mummy afraid that the tightly-drawn skin of his face might crack. 'Oh no, officer, that's what insulates me. The wood pulp stops the cancer rays from penetrating. They try and they try from out there, but all the rays keep bouncing off. As long as I keep a wall like that around me, I'll live to a hundred.' And from Sullivan's serene expression, it was plain to see that he expected to live perhaps even longer.

That did it. Blew a half-assed theory right out the window.

'See you round,' said Harry. 'Thanks for your time, Mr Sullivan.'

'No problem, officer. We'd all like it round here if you could clear that casket thing up. Mrs Johnson's driving us all crazy with her talk about it – you should see the look on Franklin's face sometimes! It's getting to us.'

Harry went back up the hall, drained and dirtied by all he hated about downtown. He caught sight of the midget scampering ahead of him, trying to avoid being near the elevator when he reached it. This only made him feel worse.

'Hey, Franklin J.!' he called out. 'Forget what I said, will ya?'

'Shit, that's OK!' squeaked Franklin J. Abercrombie, stopping and tipping his little head back to look up at him. 'I guessed you had things on your mind, so I didn't care too much. If I'd cared, I'd have socked you one, you know that? Flattened you right out on the floor!'

'You would?' said Harry, chuckling.

'You wanna try me?'

'Another time, Franklin, OK? I gotta get down to detox.'

'Sure, I can smell it on your breath from here,' said Franklin J., rising on tip-toe and sniffing.

Harry laughed and stepped into the elevator. He was getting used to the lever control, and the cage began a slow, steady descent. It was just a pity that Art wasn't riding with him to be impressed. What was that joke thing Art had been talking about the last time? A guy takes the elevator thirty floors down in the morning, and then rides up to only the eighteenth on his return, climbing the stairs the rest of the way . . . And there was a link in it with Franklin J. Abercrombie.

Suddenly, Harry remembered the punchline. The man was a midget who could reach the ground-floor button OK, but the eighteenth button was the highest he could reach on his way home again.

Then, with equal suddenness, Harry yanked the lever back the other way.

Franklin J. Abercrombie's room had to be one of the saddest places in all of downtown San Diego. If you looked closely at the red bathrobe on the hook behind the door, you could see where a bunny rabbit design had been carefully removed from it, although the label inside still read *Tinkerbell Products*. Mickey Mouse decals had been partially scraped from the lid of the tiny writing desk, and the chair that went with it was also a piece of playroom furniture. In fact the whole room was a lot like a nursery, if you ignored the double bed and counted as toys the dirty magazines and cigar butts lying about. It even smelled a little like one; a faint aroma of boiled milk and fecal matter.

'Nobody ever comes in here,' said Franklin J., reaching up to the bed to push some soiled socks tidily out of the way under the pillow. 'That's why I let it get a bit of a mess, I guess.'

'Mine's the same,' admitted Harry.

He was studying the faded piece of wine-coloured carpet. There was a less faded strip running down one side of it for about seven feet. That was where the casket must've rested. The size of the thing didn't make sense yet, but everything else fitted.

Take the so called sex-related MO. Franklin J. had simply gone for the groin area because that was as close to a vital organ as he could reach.

Take the victims' claims of having been attacked by someone invisible.

Franklin J. was the most invisible human being that Harry had ever tripped over. He could easily have hidden himself behind the small trash cans in the alley, or he could have actually been inside one of them.

Take the laughter heard by the three witnesses. Franklin J had a laugh that was high-pitched and, once you came to think about it, very girlish.

Which was to say nothing of how well he fitted the description of some 'freaky guy' who might not want anyone to know he had a casket stashed away.

Franklin J. Abercrombie cleared his throat. 'What was the important thing you wanted to discuss with me, officer?' he asked, sitting on his desk and letting his legs swing. 'As if I hadn't guessed already.'

'You have?'

'Sure, you're all nervous and sweaty. I must be your first homicide arrest.'

'Second,' corrected Harry. 'But you mean you're admitting to . . . ?'

'Sure, I was going down to the station later on to cop out anyway. I just wanted the last of those bastids to pay his dues first.'

Harry laughed. 'Goddamn,' he said, 'there goes my Special Citation!'

Franklin J. laughed too. 'You'd get a citation for solving the case? Hell, there's no need for you to lose out on that. How can I help?'

'By tellin' me all about it, I guess.'

'OK, lemme do that small thing. Not much to it, but maybe you'd better get out your notebook.'

Harry did that, and settled back as Franklin J. began to speak.

'One night, around twelve days ago, I was hangin' around on F, when a broad came up to me and we started to rap. Not many broads ever talk to me, not properly, more baby talk that makes me bad mouth 'em so they go again. Oh man, I thought, this is *it*. She seemed to really like me, for myself – understand? I spent money, I drank a *lake*, got hornier than a moose. Went back to her place and the rest I don't really remember. What I *do* remember is when I kinda crawled back here, the casket was gone. My one irreplaceable possession. You wouldn't believe me if I told you how long and how hard I had to scrimp and save for that thing! But it was gone, and I got *mad*, mad enough to kill.' He shrugged. 'So I killed.'

Harry could tell he was talking lightly over the surface of things, for his face had turned twitchy with barely contained rage and self-pity. Any questions would have to be put lightly, too.

'Sounds quite a night, Franklin. Am I right, you didn't get back here to the hotel until the mornin'?'

'Right. Arno and Masters and that other punk wanted me out of the place so they could sneak the casket into the elevator and out through the lobby while the desk clerk wasn't lookin'. They needed to pick their moment.'

'And how did you pick up on who they were?'

'I lucked out. Rikki Sullivan told me about the fight that'd gone on in the Johnsons' room, and so I found some excuse to bring the matter up with Wilma. She gave me the address on Imperial, Arno's name, and I started asking round. Pretty soon I knew who the three were – it wasn't difficult. The difficult part was making myself wait until I could get each of them alone. *Fuckin' bastids!*'

Harry was startled by the sudden shout. 'Franklin, you OK?' Then he saw that the midget was crying.

'I'm a man, a goddamn *man*,' sobbed Franklin J. Abercrombie, clutching his tiny hands to his face. 'Now what's gonna happen? When I die, I wanted it to look like a man was bein' buried – not some four-year-old kid or somethin'. I don't want the tears of old ladies! I want people to look at my casket goin' by, and to say to themselves, *My, oh my, they're buryin' a REAL MAN today.*'

Harry's final question had been answered. There could be no doubt now why the poor little sucker had wanted the biggest box money could buy. So he read him his rights and put the handcuffs on.

They met up with Sergeant Brunowski downstairs in the hotel lobby and her eyes came out on stalks.

'Harry,' she said, 'what the hell's goin' on? I'm the one who interviewed that hooker down the detox, heard how this scam was worked. *I'm* the one who was coming to make this arrest. How did you know this was the guy? And why, for Chrissakes, is he looking so *goddamn happy*?'

'There's people all around lookin' at him, Sarge.'

'Shit, I can see that – still don't make no sense.'

'Look at the cuffs he's wearin'.'

'Huh? What's so special about them?'

'They're man-sized,' said Harry.

Ellis Peters

COME TO DUST

My wife's Aunt Filomena is the oldest of a big family, of which Fran's Mum is the youngest, and I reckon there must be twenty years between them. The old girl's all of seventy-five now, but indestructible, and in her time she's run through three marriages, one divorce and two widowhoods, the second one highly profitable. But for that, she might have been having a look round now for her fourth, but ending up with half a million, even in dollars, has tipped the scale in favour of settling back into solitary luxury and putting her feet up. She's holed up in California, and not likely to do much cavorting about the world any more, but she's lost none of her volcanic energy, or her genius for disrupting the affairs of her scattered family from a distance.

That side of Fran's family comes from Turin. Her Mum's name, before she married an Englishman over on business, was Emilia Cecchini, and the Italian influence remained dominant. All the Cecchinis are born managers and administrators. North Italians are like that, not small, dark and private, like south of Eboli, where Christianity stopped, but big, assertive and blonde, everything the Italians are not supposed to be. Moreover, by instinct they sing in harmony, just like small dark Welshmen, while the small dark southerners, who physically resemble Welshmen, are despairingly monodic to the last forlorn degree. How do you make sense of that?

To get back to Aunt Filomena, the doyenne of the lot. In her affluent retirement, with a married son not far away, money

137

enough to buy all the attendance she wants, and no worries, she has developed a new hobby. Hobby? Obsession! She keeps a family tree complete with all the third and fourth generation, all but herself and Cousin Paolo left behind here in Britain and Europe, mostly in Italy. And she loves to buy presents for this one and that one, as the fit takes her. She's the wealthiest of the bunch, and granted she's generous, she loves to spread the joy. With the kids she does pretty well. Maybe she's in her second childhood, and understands what children like. With the rest of us she has a marvellous knack of discovering white elephants.

The trouble is, she has got hooked on auctioneers' catalogues, and has them sent to her in advance from all the main houses, goes through them with eyeballs bulging, picks out the most appalling specimens of expensive kitsch, and despatches her orders to agents wherever the sales are taking place, London, Zurich, New York, Amsterdam, Florence – you name it! – to bid for the most God-awful pieces, provided they're labelled 'important', which means fashionable and hellishly expensive. Then she has them sent to such relatives as she feels would best both love and deserve them.

I am never sure whether this is pure, misguided benevolence, or plain mischief.

Anyhow, that's how we happened to get Aunt Filomena's nineteenth century copy of an (alleged!) earlier French *bonheur du jour* delivered to our unoffending bungalow in a quarter of an acre, in the second-best district of our prosperous and genteel market town, as a birthday present to Fran.

You have never, but never, seen such a monstrosity. Its only admirer throughout has been the long-haired nit who helped the driver to lift it inside. He thought it was wonderful. Afterwards we wished we'd asked for his name and address, he could have given it to his old Mum for a Christmas present. The driver was a pro who regularly delivered for the firm, he averted his eyes as he helped to carry it in. He was accustomed to the better trade. If he said six words during the whole transaction, that was about it. He accelerated away from our gate as if he feared we might call him back to take the thing away before he could escape.

So there it stood in our hall, out in the open to be viewed from every side, and Fran and I circled warily round it looking for a place from which it might look better, but there wasn't one. There wasn't a prospect that pleased. Like man, the thing was vile.

A *bonheur du jour* is, or should be, a lady's writing-desk, where she is supposed to sit down in the morning, full of housewifely energy and importance, to write her letters, her menus for the day, and any notes she may think necessary, perhaps her diary, too, if she has a bent that way. Mostly the French ones were light, elegant and decorative in a graceful, restrained way. This thing was bloated, heavy, with two tiers of drawers, on either side a kneehole, and one long, shallow drawer above the knee-space; and above the writing surface a raised back panel flanked by two more very small drawers.

It wasn't simply that it was covered all over with ornamentation that bore no relationship to its shape, but mainly that the shape itself was all wrong. Every proportion was false by just that fraction that turned it into horrid caricature. The ornamentation was a bonus. All its edges, pedestals and writing surface alike, were finished with frills, like okra pods – no, more like some obscene lizard; and all its surfaces except the back were inlaid with vari-coloured veneers and bits of coloured glass in intricate patterns. I won't say every small oblong had a different design – I daresay they ran out of ideas here and there, and slipped in a duplicate – but certainly there was no pattern or symmetry in their arrangement. As a finishing touch, all the frills were gilded at the edges. And there it sat and leered at us.

'And I shall be expected to write and *thank* her for it!' Fran said, bitterly but resignedly.

What can you do? Kith and kin are kith and kin, and you can't deliberately hurt their feelings. Everybody who's ever had a most unwelcome present delivered in good faith knows the procedure. The difficulty is to sound cheerfully grateful without going overboard into such fulsome appreciation that it defeats its own end. But Fran has a warm corner for Aunt Filomena, and a kind heart, and she manages to make it ring true.

Well, we may have looked our gift horse very dubiously in the mouth, but at least we did make an honest effort to find a suitable stable for it. The note that came with it gave a full description but a vague and incomplete provenance. The thing had, like so many nineteenth-century pieces, two concealed drawers, hardly worth calling secret, since a seven-year-old could have found his way in, once informed there was something there to be found, but private enough unless you knew they were there. They were built into the tops of the two pedestals, and all you had to do was to open the visible top drawer, slip your fingers inside the top of it, press up a tilted slip of wood there, and draw it forward, and out popped a section of the apparently solid inlay immediately under the writing surface, to reveal another shallow drawer. When you pushed it in again the wooden catch clicked home and fastened it closed, and the awful expanse of inlay showed complete again.

Fran made a determined effort to take it seriously and make use of it. 'It's meant for writing on,' she said, 'and I'll use it for writing. If we have to give it house-room, let's make it earn its keep.'

She moved all her notepaper, envelopes, pens, ink and what have you into the drawers, all very orderly and neat. She even insisted on using the secret drawers, all her pens and pencils, stapler and stamp-book in the left-hand one, her bottles of blue and red ink in the right. I forget how we even came to have red ink, I think it must have been when I was map-making for a client at the office. Anyhow, Fran stood it for fully three weeks before she gave up. That thing was the wrong height for writing on, no matter what chair or stool you used, the desk wouldn't accommodate her typewriter, and the frilly edge was hideously uncomfortable under the wrist for writing by hand.

So then we tried the most obscure corner of the living-room, but it wasn't obscure enough, the thing managed to obtrude ominously wherever we parked it. Then we stuck it out in the hall, where at least we weren't obliged to look at it all the time, but it still contrived to get in the way, and Fran said it grinned at her every time she passed it.

I don't know why it took us so long to realise that we weren't forced to go on enduring the thing. Aunt Filomena had long ago had her letter of thanks, and was some thousands of miles away in California, and never likely to cross the Atlantic again, so how was she ever to know whether we continued to cherish her gift, or threw it out thankfully and forgot about it? Where ignorance is bliss . . . Of course she'd never know!

'Do you really think we could?' wondered Fran, brightening at the very thought. 'I'd feel mean, somehow, if we sold it. All I want is to get rid of it, not to turn it to profit. If we gave it away I shouldn't feel quite so base.'

It was getting round into December then, and our annual riot of fund-raising events for the mayor's great Christmas charity appeal was in full swing, so I said why not donate Aunt Filomena's *bonheur du jour* to the Lions' auction for the good cause. And we did.

Nobody bid for it.

Tommy Anslow, who ran the do, said he thought it was too upstage for his customers, and it was a shame, really, not to put so remarkable a piece into its own kind of sale, and we'd better take it back for the present. So we did.

Well, if we couldn't get any of our respectable neighbours to take it, we could throw it open to the less respectable. *Somebody* had to have that sort of taste, surely. So we did what we'd done once or twice before when we installed new furniture and wanted to get rid of the old, we put the thing out by the gate, with a notice saying: *If you fancy this, please take it and welcome*.

It had always worked before. Things vanished like magic. Not this time. After some days it snowed, so we took it in again as far as the porch. In a proper house it could have been hoisted out of sight into the attic long before then, but modern bungalows don't have attics. It was still in the porch, like an astronaut stuck in the air-lock, when Ben and Meg came to spend Christmas with us.

Ben is Fran's younger brother, and where girls are concerned more Italian than the Italians. He is also a dealer in antiques, prints and ceramics mostly, though he does a little with furniture, too, when he drops on something he likes. He wasn't going to like Aunt Filomena's writing-desk, that was for sure.

And now I suppose you're thinking in terms of Frances and Benjamin for these two half-breeds? Not a bit of it. She's Francesca, and he's Benedetto. I told you the Italian side was dominant. Ben is elegant, handsome and promiscuous, at least as far as eyes and tongue are concerned, but dead practical, too, and had the sense to marry Meg, his girl-Friday, who knows as much about prints as he does, and almost as much about ceramics. Meg is thin, plain, exquisitely dressed on next to nothing, with a sardonic turn of speech, and the cool nerves any woman with a wandering-eyed husband needs. She is imperturbable, with good reason. She knows not only that Ben will always come back, but also that he'll always come back with renewed pleasure.

The pair of them took one look at the exile in the air-lock. Meg continued to study it with detached interest. Ben closed his eyes and shuddered.

'What,' he demanded, with his eyes still closed, 'is that?'

'That,' said Fran, almost smug in her despair, 'is Aunt Filomena's *bonheur du jour*, and my last birthday present from her.'

Ben opened one eye, cautiously, and closed it again. Meg said: 'More of a *malheur du jour*, wouldn't you say?'

Ben said at once, as soon as he could get both eyes open: 'Get rid of it! No one can be asked to live with that. I don't care if it did come from Aunt Filomena. She's never going to erupt on your doorstep, and what the eye doesn't see the heart doesn't grieve. Get rid of it!'

Over drinks, over dinner, over the first far too early carol singers elbowing and giggling on the doorstep, we explained that we'd already tried to get rid of it, without success. It kept coming back like a song. Or like garlic!

'You've got a bulk-garbage disposal arrangement of some sort,' said Ben ruthlessly, 'you must have. Every council has. What's that thing but bulk-garbage? Chuck it out, before it turns you peculiar. No use being sentimental where your sanity's at stake.'

It took a bit of getting used to, but I could see Fran warming to the idea. And Meg said placidly: 'She was cheated, anyhow, I'll bet. It isn't worth even its curiosity price. Much better let her dream she gave you something precious, if eccentric. She's never going to know any better, is she?'

We were coming up to the last pre-Christmas visit from the bin-boys then, and we looked at each other, and visibly thought, well, why not?

Our friendly neighbourhood dustman is a glorious patriarch by the name of Augustus, believe it or not. He isn't, of course, our only dustman, he's the gaffer of the regular squad, and the monarch of our local tip, which he keeps with the strict neatness and precision of a Puritan prelate. Which he almost is, for he's a local preacher of an elder school, too benevolent for hell-fire, rather of the 'Lord-knock-a-brick-out-and-let-glory-in!' persuasion. Even in orange overalls he has a regal look about him. In visage he's weather-beaten and benign, with grizzled, wiry hair, and a five o'clock shadow that begins to manifest itself around noon. In build he's stocky and powerful, and composed entirely of right angles, as befits so foursquare a character. And like all the delivery and service men around the town, he's on terms of warm mutual respect with Fran. Fran elicits Christian names as an expert waiter draws corks, with no effort at all.

'And they're due tomorrow,' said Fran, delighted. 'The last collection before Christmas.' They're not allowed to ask for Christmas boxes, but she always manages to slip them one, and usually has a glass of something warming and a mince-pie handy.

So Augustus came in and viewed the family incubus thoughtfully over his mince-pie, and gave judgement.

'I tell you what,' he said, 'I'll have it took up to the tip for you, and pop it under cover there, where folks who come to dump stuff can see it, and it'll be out of the weather, and we'll see what happens. You'd be surprised how folks who wouldn't give things another look on a market stall or put out by a gate, like you put this, will pounce on 'em and haul 'em away like treasure when they find 'em on the tip. Some of what gets fetched away that road we get back later, when they come to their right senses. But the thought of picking up something for nothing, and having *discovered* it, as you might say . . . They get carried away. No reason why something that's no good to you shouldn't be some good to someone else, is there? When I get something that might catch somebody's eye, I let it lie in full view a few days, and as often as not it gets fetched away.'

All of which we already knew, though we'd never expected to have to take advantage of it. Our local tip is a decorous distance out of town, among open fields, covering a large plot of waste ground that's been pitted with old surface mining and earlier shallow shafts. They're gradually levelling it off, and the first quarter or so is already smoothed and tidied and under grass, and there Augustus and his myrmidons have a hut, and a large covered port for lorries and plant while on the job, and that's where he puts such cast-off objects as he thinks worthy of survival if some inquisitive visitor fancies them. I go there sometimes to take massive loads of hedge-brushings or other garden rubbish, and it's quite amazing what people do throw away. No wonder some of it gets reclaimed by more thrifty-minded people. Not that I could imagine anyone falling upon our contribution with glad cries. But they could always bulldoze it in, if all else failed.

'You don't know how grateful I'll be,' said Fran fervently, 'to see the back of it. Will it be all right if we drive it round there tomorrow?'

'Bless you, ma'am, no need for that,' said Augustus. 'I've got a van coming round this way this afternoon. My lads will pick it up on their way out there.'

It seemed his lads were a somewhat motley lot at the time, due to a 'flu bug that was running round the district in full cry. So many of the regulars were down with it that he'd had to take on some casuals, a scratch lot including a few students not too proud to take a dirty holiday job. He admitted they weren't doing too badly. Certainly the pair who called to pick up the *bonheur du jour* in the afternoon seemed brisk and willing enough. One dark young fellow, and one fair, in borrowed orange overalls. They eyed the thing with interest, and didn't say no to a mince-pie each. Fran was so happy to be getting shot of the horror that she never stopped talking. She even demonstrated one of the 'secret' drawers and how to open and shut it, the left-hand one, from which she'd long since removed her pens and stamps and stapler. They were fascinated. They popped their fingers in, pressed the catch, sprang the drawer open and clicked it shut several times, ran a finger along the almost invisible join, and remarked, truly, that whether you liked the thing or not, a lot of fairly expert work had gone into it. Which is true of a lot of artifacts which had better never have been started at all, but are put together to last almost for ever.

'Just the job, that,' said the fair one, 'for keeping your diamond studs in.'

'Or your love letters,' offered the dark one. He was showing the usual reaction to Fran, and I wouldn't swear he hadn't one eye on Meg, too, who may not be so obviously decorative, but draws plenty of male eyes, all the same. 'You're sure you want to part with it?'

Fran said yes, emphatically she did, and never to see it again. And with that they seized it boisterously, hoisted it, and galloped out jauntily to stow it in their van, and off it went at last. We closed the door on it, and heaved a concerted sigh of content at seeing the last of it.

145

'Students!' said Meg reflectively, having weighed up our deliverers as she watched them depart. 'Now I wonder what those two are studying? Womankind, to judge by the dark one's roving eye. Such a bright blue eye, too. I saw it wink at you, Fran.'

'So did I!' admitted Fran. 'Do you think I overdid the grace and charm? I was so darned pleased to see them, I suppose I practically fawned. Even when Augustus promised, I could hardly believe I was really going to be rid of that awful thing. It's a wonder I didn't kiss the pair of them, I'm so grateful.'

'Be grateful to Augustus,' I said. 'I don't know that I'd mind you kissing him – just once at New Year, maybe, for auld lang syne. It would be worth it to see his face.'

'Good-looking lad, though,' said Meg thoughtfully, 'that dark one. Well, now we can all breathe more easily. And Aunt Filomena just as happy as ever!'

It's quite extraordinary how much more spacious the house seemed without that lumpish nuisance. We went back to our Christmas preparations with lighter hearts, and Ben and Meg set off on their round of friendly calls in the neighbourhood, and left us to it. There were three more fund-raising events the day before Christmas Eve, and then the gala concert and supper on Christmas Eve itself, where all the takings would be handed in to Roddy Hughes, who is treasurer. I avoid committees like the plague, but Fran is on the Ladies' Committee, and inevitably gets roped in among the voluntary helpers, catering, selling tickets and programmes, serving the buffet supper and what have you. Even lady guests of our committee women are drafted unless they're good at dodging. Meg is excellent at dodging. She says it would cramp Ben's style if she occupied a place anywhere but in the discreet background on social occasions.

You know what these do's are like, they must be much the same everywhere, with all the local talent competing for a place on the programme. The male voice choir sings, the chamber orchestra plays, the best of the amateur and semi-professional

singers bring out their ballads and duets, and the evening ends
with a grand carol-sing led by the Town Hall organ, which
happens to be quite a good one. As the bar is open well before
the performance begins, and for a half-hour interval midway,
we can sing like nobody's business by the finish, and a good
time is had by all. It's a very dressy occasion, too, which adds to
the pleasure for the eyes.

Fran went along early to sell programmes and help organise
the buffet, and then joined us before the show began. Ben
fought his way to the bar for drinks for Meg and himself – I was
driving – and came back with his chin on his shoulder and a
thoughtful look in his eye.

'Who's the blonde in the blue dress?' he asked Fran when she
joined us. 'Behind the bar. Local girl? I don't remember her last
year.'

There were two or three girls helping the professional
barman behind the bar, all volunteers, all young and attractive.
Evidently one of them had already taken Ben's critical eye. No
beating about the bush with Ben, he goes straight for what he
wants.

'Oh, that one!' said Meg. 'I was wondering which of them it
would be. Not bad, not bad at all!'

'I don't know her name,' said Fran. 'I think she came with
Mrs Grant.' Mrs Grant is the secretary of the Ladies'
Committee, and quite capable of recruiting any young female
relative who happens to be spending Christmas with her. 'They
arrived together. Probably a niece or something. I don't
remember her from last year, either, and yet I do feel I've seen
her somewhere before. She *is* fetching, isn't she?'

The girl was just abandoning her bottles and glasses and
emerging to go into the hall and take her seat. The blue dress
was floor-length and fluted from the hips, long-sleeved and high
at the neck, very demure indeed. Her hair was almost
primrose-fair, and cut short in a smooth, feathery style that set
off good cheekbones and a wide forehead, and eyes, viewed at
that distance, several shades darker than the blue of her gown.

Not bad at all! There were plenty of fluffier, fancier, more elaborately dressed girls around, but Ben goes for quality and style.

There was no pursuing her then, it was time to take our places. But when the first half had gone off smoothly and we came out for the interval, there she was behind the bar again, and somehow, as soon as Ben and I had provided our womenfolk with their chosen poison, Ben was lost again.

By that time Roddy Hughes had the ticket and door takings all corralled, plus the three sums handed in from the previous night's fund-raising events, and was shut up with a couple of helpers in the office at the rear of the hall, feverishly totting up the lot and committing it to the office safe in its locked bag, since there'd be no banking it until after the two-day holiday. The takings from the bar and the sale of raffle tickets would have to wait to be totalled up separately afterwards. Everybody was already acquiring a smug glow of virtue at duty done. Ben's blonde girl emerged from the bar with a tray of drinks for the backroom boys and a black coffee for Roddy, who loses his ability to add up after even a mild dose of alcohol. And guess who loped gracefully ahead to open all the doors for her and escort her back again, blushing. There were rivals in the field by then, but they were up against something out of their class.

Meg smiled and said: 'Not to worry, he thrives on competition. It's competition that keeps him safe, and confirms his judgement at the same time. You don't suppose he really wants anything to come of it, do you, beyond a perfume and a rose-leaf? It's a *clair-de-lune* thing, a *fête galante* thing. He dances to an imaginary mirror. So – I hope! – does she. Though she does look a bit young and innocent for it,' she ended doubtfully.

I don't think she need have worried, the blue girl, shy and quiet though she might be, was clearly enjoying herself and well able to cope. Ben rejoined us for the second half not displeased with his own image, but disapproving strongly of the boisterous attentions of one or two of our local young bloods. They tend to get a little above themselves on such occasions. Didn't we all, once?

It was pretty plain that Ben had his private plans to corner the girl at supper, after we'd all sung ourselves hoarse and sufficiently admired the sound of our own voices. In the milling throng ferrying their plates hungrily along the buffet tables I did catch a glimpse of the primrose-coloured head once or twice, but by the time we'd stacked our plates and picked up our wine and found a reasonably protected corner from which to survey the scrum in comparative safety, I'd completely lost her. Worse, so had Ben. He's taller than most of us, but even with that advantage he'd begun to wear a frown of mingled frustration and concern. He slipped away back to the buffet, with a sharp eye cocked either way as he went, to check on those who came late, or went back for refills or more wine, but no girl. Cinderella had left before the end of the ball, wiser than in the fairy tale.

'And I don't see that clot who was pestering her in the interval, either,' said Ben, vexed. 'I hope she hasn't gone off with him. I wouldn't trust him as far as I could throw him.'

'If she came with Mrs Grant,' said Fran reasonably, 'she'll have left with Mrs Grant, and I know *she* left as soon as she'd had a word with Roddy Hughes and seen the records and the money into the safe.'

So that's how the evening ended. We all went home about midnight, and more or less shut the business of the world out for the next two days. You know how it is at Christmas. No newspapers, the news on telly and radio cut down to size, and nobody bothers to turn it on, anyhow. No offices to attend, no banks to deposit in or borrow from, no business letters to answer, no nothing to spoil the calm. Except that Ben, still preoccupied, took himself off on Christmas morning for a walk, and went to church instead. He came back considerably aggrieved, and confronted Fran with: 'I thought you said that girl was staying with Mrs Grant.'

'I said she arrived with Mrs Grant,' said Fran, interested. 'Why? Isn't she?'

'I had a word with Mrs Grant after church,' said Ben with dignity. 'Wished her the usual, asked if she was tired after last night – you know the line.' No one can shoot it better with middle-aged ladies. 'Then I asked if her guest had enjoyed the gala. *What guest?* So then I had to describe her. She's nothing whatever to do with the Grants. Mrs Grant thought she was with Mrs Forster.'

'So then,' said Meg, sweetly smiling, 'I suppose you passed the compliments of the season with Mrs Forster. No dice?'

'Mrs Forster,' said Ben flatly, 'thought she was with Fran. Nice, helpful girl, but never seen her in her life before.'

'And yet I still feel that *I* have, somewhere, some time,' said Fran, after the subject had otherwise been dropped, even by Ben, though he was still brooding.

The day after Boxing Day, usually slow and reluctant to start up again, actually went off like a bomb that time. Two bombs! For when Roddy Hughes went to the Town Hall in the morning to collect his big leather bag of money and take it to the bank, unlocking the door of the office, unlocking the door of the safe, and fingering forth his little key to unlock the bag itself, quite unnecessarily, for the pure pleasure of taking a look at all that delectable loot, he found he had no lock in which to insert it, no bag, no money, nothing on the shelf. Admitted it was an old safe a seven-year-old could probably have opened, if ever it had entered his head to try, but nobody had ever questioned its security before, and until now nobody had robbed it.

The sensation ran round the town like wildfire. The second bomb made no great noise anywhere but in our bungalow, but there it drowned out the other. It was a letter from Aunt Filomena in California. Cousin Paolo, she wrote, had had to fly over to Turin on family business, and he proposed to return via London, and come and spend a few days with us in the New Year before flying home. And she had asked him to bring back up-to-date photographs of us all, and of the house. In particular she looked forward to seeing how her *bonheur du jour* had fitted into our home.

In panic and recrimination we wasted at least ten minutes, everyone accusing everyone else of stupidly urging the jettisoning of the thing, on the grounds that Aunt Filomena would never know, when there were so many ways in which she might find out. Then Fran said: 'Shut up, and *do* something! We know where it is, don't we? It can just as easily come back, can't it? There's only one thing to be done, take the station wagon and go and fetch it.'

'It's been out in the weather for a week,' I said feebly. 'And how if somebody's adopted it and made off with it? That's what we wanted to happen.'

'Ha!' said Fran scornfully. She knew it better than that. 'It'll still be there, where Augustus put it, and he said under cover. Get going!'

So Ben and I leaped into the station wagon and drove off to the tip to retrieve the horrid thing.

Our tip must have the biggest inland resident colony of seagulls anywhere short of the central European breeding grounds. They live there all the year, doing a useful job of scavenging and tidying up the area, but you have to watch your heads when you drive in through the gate to the edge of the levelled and grassed part, because at the sound of a car they go up in their thousands like a snowstorm in reverse.

Augustus came out of his hut just as we pulled up. He had a grievance of his own, because the usual had happened, and half his squad who should have shown up for work that morning were stretching the holiday a little – possibly only for this one day, but he darkly suspected some of them wouldn't clock in again until after New Year. It was an old human failing, and Augustus accepted it in a spirit of Christian resignation. One of his temporaries, at any rate, had shown up for work, for the fair boy who had helped to remove the writing-desk emerged from the hut to help us reload it. No doubt he thought we were looney, but we didn't bother to explain to him. We did to

Augustus, after he'd led us to the spot where the thing lurked, as evil as ever, and none the worse (or better!) for its stay among the garbage.

'Well, it's worth a little self-sacrifice to keep the lady happy,' he said gravely. 'And probably the gentleman won't be visiting this way for some years, after this.' It was kind of him to point out so soothingly that our suffering need only be temporary. 'It would be a shame to wound her feelings, when she meant it as a generous act.' And he looked up rather warily into the sky full of seagulls and threatening frost or snow, and murmured: '– thou dost not bite so nigh, as benefits forgot!' You can always rely on Augustus to have a line of Shakespeare ready for most occasions.

We hoisted the horror into the station wagon, and drove back home as if we expected Cousin Paolo to be on the doorstep ahead of us. We parked the desk dubiously in the least offensive position in the living-room, and Fran drew a finger along the top and decided that we ought to polish it up a bit after its week in the cold and the dust. That was when she opened the top pedestal drawer on the right, to wipe away the rim of dust left where it didn't fit flush, and let out a yell of pure surprise that brought us all crowding round.

The drawer wasn't empty, as it had been, but full of crumpled blue fabric that looked like silk jersey. Meg leaned and plucked it out, and it uncoiled in her hands into the unmistakable shape of a full-length dress, high-necked and long-sleeved, dirty now and creased, and with a great, blackening reddish stain all over breast and shoulder.

Ben was the first to recognise it. He gave a yelp of horror, and grabbed it away from Meg. 'My God, whatever . . . This is *hers*! Look at it! It's the dress that girl was wearing on Christmas Eve. For God's sake, what's happened to her?'

'You're crazy!' snapped Meg, rather fending off belief than expressing any real doubt. 'It's just a dress someone threw away. Why should it be hers?'

'It *is*!' Ben insisted. 'I'd know it again anywhere. That poor kid . . .'

'It is,' Fran echoed him hollowly. 'Look here!' And she plucked a pale, smooth hair from the shoulder of the dress, and even the hair was dark at one end from whatever had dried there.

Ben fell upon the other three drawers and dragged them out, to reveal a few more pathetic relics hurriedly shoved into hiding there, a long white evening slip, a pair of silver-grey nylon hold-ups, the kind of stockings that need no suspender belt, and a soiled and draggled lacy bra with one broken shoulder-strap.

'Hers!' said Ben hoarsely. 'They must be . . .'

We stood and gaped at the wretched little collection, all spoiled and befouled as they were, and couldn't choose but think of the wearer, perhaps similarly violated and abandoned, there among the garbage.

'Let everything lie,' said Ben after a long silence. 'This is police business now. That . . .' He stabbed a finger at the ominous blackish red stain, dried into a crust at the edges. '*That* – is blood. Don't mess with these things any more than we already have, just leave them. Bill, you'd better . . .'

'I know,' I said, and made for the telephone to dial 999.

They came, first Sergeant Green, whom we all knew, and later an inspector and others. We had to tell them the whole story of how the *bonheur du jour* had been banished and then hurriedly fished back again. What we'd found inside we didn't have to tell them, every item was there to be seen, and by that time we were all quite certain of the girl who had last been seen wearing them. But there was nothing more we could tell them about the girl herself, except that so far we hadn't found anyone who knew who she was, or where she'd come from.

'It does look,' said Sergeant Green, 'as if we've got something worse than a robbery on our hands now. Queer we should get two such cases dropped on us together, a quiet place like this. Though if there's any connection between the two, so far I don't see it.'

They put every article of clothing carefully into a plastic bag, picked a few more short fair hairs from the neck of the dress, noted that the zipper at the back was wrenched out of place, as though the dress had been torn off her by force, and went off with everything to get forensic reports, and to interview Augustus and get him to show them exactly where the desk had been standing while it remained at the tip. The few taciturn remarks they exchanged in our hearing gave little away, except that they were taking the matter very seriously.

'No pants, you notice. No vest or anything – if they wear them under this sort of gear. It was a cold night.'

'Could be still on the body.'

'No coat, but it would be bulky, and if she was wearing fur it would be worth making off with, of course.'

We hadn't seen whatever coat she'd been wearing, but the cloakroom that night had been bulging with furs.

'And no shoes. If there was a struggle she may have lost those. We'll look for them on the spot.'

'Some devil dragged her in there,' Ben said bitterly, 'and then raped and killed her. Maybe she had to take that road past the tip to get home . . . Maybe this chap offered to escort her, and then . . .'

They didn't say anything to that. But that same day they began to search the tip, the whole great, unpleasant slope of it, where tipping was currently going on, where a body could most easily be covered from view. If her clothes were there, she couldn't be far away.

And still, though the whole town was boiling now with rumours, and everyone who had attended the gala was being questioned, still nobody could say who she was, or where she'd come from. Nor where she'd gone to, either. They had bulldozers carefully turning up the recent layers, and policemen wading among the debris, and dogs, and every resource you can think of, but they didn't find the blonde girl, nor her missing shoes. Augustus looked on with sorrowful dignity, shook his head, and murmured something about 'golden lads and girls all must . . .' But he didn't like seeing his beautiful orderly tip either used for such vile purposes as murder, or so torn to pieces by the law.

But if they didn't find a body, they did find the leather bag in which Roddy Hughes had locked the entire proceeds of all our charity events. Still locked – it was the one lock which had defeated the thief. But empty, of course. He'd used a knife to slit it open, and he was now between seven and eight hundred pounds richer than he'd been ten days previously, and in mixed, easily usable currency, too. But if there was plain sign that the thief had been here, did that also prove him the murderer? There's a lot of our town dump, it looked like being a very long job sifting all of it.

In the end it turned out not to be necessary.

It was two days later when Sergeant Green came to see us again, and asked if he could take another look at our *bonheur du jour*.

'You see,' said he mildly, 'we've now had the forensic reports on those clothes, and there are several interesting things to note. To begin with – that dark stain on the dress. I don't know if you noticed that there wasn't a mark on the slip she wore under it. That stain isn't blood, after all. It turns out it's red ink.'

'Red *ink*?' echoed Fran, wide-eyed; and suddenly she gave a sort of strangled squeak, and plunged upon Aunt Filomena's gift, and plucked open the top pedestal drawer on the right side. 'Of *course*! Since ball-pens I hardly ever use even blue ink, let alone red. When they fetched this away I clean forgot . . .'

She sprang the catch and hauled open the shallow drawer hidden above. Two ink-bottles rolled ponderously about the space within. The blue ink had had its cap screwed on firmly enough to remain sealed while rattled along in the van, but the red had not, and its entire contents had dyed the base of the drawer, and seeped through the seams to drip steadily into the drawer below, providing a puddle into which the crumpled dress had been stuffed in a hurry. When it was heaved about, the bottles had fallen over, the motion of the van had kept them rolling, and worked off the loose cap.

'Then *no blood*!' breathed Fran, and looked up hopefully at Sergeant Green. 'So it may not be as bad as we feared?'

'Well,' said Sergeant Green deprecatingly, 'there's also the matter of the fair hairs. There were three or four caught in the zipper, as it happens. That jammed it, that's why it had to be ripped apart by force to get the dress off. And as it turns out – they're not hairs at all – well, not human hairs. They're nylon. So I thought, if I may have another look at where everything was stowed . . . And that little trick you just did, ma'am – would there be another like it this other side?'

Fran was staring at Meg and Meg was staring at Fran, and their mouths and eyes hung wide open, and there was some frantic reassessment going on inside their heads. And then they both began to speak at once.

'Fran – it was the *left* one you showed them . . .'

Fran stared through her, and said: 'I *said* I kept thinking I'd seen her before . . .'

'A blue and roving eye,' said Meg in a faint voice.

'Those two were the only ones I showed how to open them . . .'

Then Ben and I caught the infection, and started connecting, too, and that didn't make things much clearer for anyone listening. Ben said: 'The fair lad's there all right, he helped us load . . .'

I said: 'I'll bet the other is one of the defaulters. Augustus can tell us.'

The whole discussion didn't seem to be getting anywhere, or providing much enlightenment for Sergeant Green, so Fran pounced on the left-hand pedestal, opened the upper drawer, slid in her fingers and sprang the catch.

There were just three things in the secret drawer she had demonstrated for Augustus's young men: a smooth, blonde, feather-cut nylon wig, and two buxom falsies to pad out the bra.

He'd worn his own underwear, of course, and the long-skirted, fluted dress, dexterously managed, was perfectly adequate to hide his shoes. He'd probably have taken the dress away with him if he hadn't wrecked the zipper getting it off.

He never clocked on for work with the bin-boys again, naturally. They tried to trace him by the clothes, but it was no go. Nobody in this town has set eyes on him since, and I doubt if anybody ever will.

Cousin Paolo never showed up, after all, he rang up from Heathrow to say that an urgent business deal had cropped up in New York, and he couldn't afford to let it slip through his fingers, so he was taking an immediate connection for home. Next year, perhaps, he said.

Augustus has smoothed out all the nasty holes and furrows the police made in his nice, tidy tip, and put out of sight, among other eyesores, Aunt Filomena's *bonheur du jour*. Henceforth cousins from California, if they ever do turn up, will have to take us as they find us – hospitable but defiant.

Ben has gone off blondes.

Miles Tripp

FORM

A man, his eyes closed in light sleep, lay in a sandy hollow among dunes which stretched behind a shingle beach. It was a warm and wind-free afternoon in October and when he had fallen asleep there had been silence except for the sighing rhythm of breaking waves and occasional cries of sea birds. He came suddenly awake to the sound of voices. Every faculty alert, he rolled over on to his stomach and crawled to the top of the ridge surrounding the dune. Cautiously he reached out to part blades of tough marram grass so that he could peer through to the next dune.

He saw a dark-haired man of about forty who wore a grey jacket, blue singlet, grey slacks, green socks and sandals. The watcher had never seen this man before but there was something in the pallor of his face and his movements, as though he needed space, which was familiar. Seated beside him was a girl of about fourteen, her fair hair in bunches, pretty and pert, blue-eyed and smiling.

How long had they been there?

As the watcher looked he saw the other man tip back a tin can and hold it up so that the last few drops fell into his wide open mouth. But some drops missed and fell on his chin. The girl laughed. The other man laughed. 'Empty,' he said, and he threw the can away. 'Let's go to my car and get another. You'd like another Coke, wouldn't you?'

The girl's laughter faded and an expression of uncertainty clouded her face. 'I don't know,' she said. 'I should be getting home.'

'It won't take a minute,' the man wheedled. 'We can come back here or I'll drive you home. Whatever you'd like.'

'All right.'

Both stood up and brushed sand from their clothes. The girl was wearing blue jeans and a white T-shirt with the word 'Cliff' in red on the front.

Stealthily (he was used to being hunted) the watcher crawled to another dune from where he could follow the progress of the couple who had disturbed his sleep. His concern wasn't because he felt threatened but on account of the girl who obviously didn't know the man well, if at all.

He saw them scramble up a low cliff to where a red Cortina was parked at the end of a track. For a few moments they were two figures against the skyline. Then the man opened the car door. A sudden struggle. A scream. The watcher leapt to his feet and began running towards the car but he tripped on an exposed root of sand sedge and fell. When he recovered, the car was being driven away at speed.

He looked around at a deserted landscape and seascape. He had been the only witness to an abduction.

It wasn't often that the three companions had time or opportunity to sit down together in the evening to relax. Boarding kennels and a dog breeding business occupied most of their waking moments. Each had an area of responsibility. Victoria, thirty-seven, well-built, blunt in speech, unconcerned to seem feminine, was the boss. She dealt with customers and was in charge of breeding, aiming always to improve stock by selection of appropriate bitches and studs. Sylvia, with whom she had set up business, was small, a gentle and composed woman who knew exactly when to assert herself against her apparently more dominant partner. She was the power behind the boss, kept the kennel-record books and undertook the considerable amount of secretarial work which the business involved. She was also in charge of domestic arrangements.

Form

The third member of the establishment was Steve, aged twenty-eight, a refugee from society who had been rescued by Victoria rather as if she had adopted a stray from a Terrier Emergency Care Scheme. He undertook menial jobs, kennel cleaning, dog exercising and anything needing heavy manual labour. The three lived in a harmony free from the sexual involvements which might have occurred when one man and two women shared the same living quarters in an isolated bungalow.

They were in the living-room watching the BBC news on television. Sylvia was mending a torn overall, Victoria cradling a glass of whisky in big brown hands, and Steve rolling himself a cigarette when an item about a missing schoolgirl was screened. Police were concerned for the safety of eleven-year-old Sandra Willingham who had disappeared while on an errand for her mother. She had been sent to a neighbour's house half a mile away to borrow a packet of tea but had never returned. An appeal was made for anyone who might have seen her to come forward. A picture of a smiling girl was flashed on to the screen. Her hair was in bunches and she wore a T-shirt with the word 'Cliff' emblazoned across its front.

Steve, about to lick wafer-thin paper, froze with the tip of his tongue between his teeth. Only eleven! She had looked much older.

'What's the matter, Steve,' asked Sylvia. 'You look as if you've seen a ghost.'

'Oh, nothin',' he mumbled and quickly resumed making a cigarette.

'You're all right?'

'Fine.'

'Quiet, you two,' intervened Victoria in a gruff voice. 'Weather!'

Steve was glad of the reprieve. The weather forecast was sacrosanct.

A high pressure belt was stationary over the eastern part of the country and the good weather likely to continue.

'In that case,' said Victoria, 'we'll do a bit of stripping and shampooing outside tomorrow. Get that foot-shy Scottie done before mistress comes to collect him on Thursday.' She stood up. 'No one wants this now,' she announced and she switched off the television without waiting for a response.

An old liver-and-white spaniel which had been lying near her feet got up and stretched stiffly. It went everywhere with Victoria and slept on the end of her bed.

'Not time yet, old girl,' said Victoria in the tender voice she reserved for the dog. For Steve, now lighting his cigarette, she used her normal deep tones. 'Tomorrow, Steve, will you take a look at the fencing at the end of the paddock. I think it needs reinforcing.'

'Sure. Will do.'

'Good lad.'

'Good lad' was the expression she always used when a dog had behaved well, but Steve didn't mind being addressed like this. At their first meeting Victoria had made it plain she preferred dogs to people. This had been shortly after her car had come to a halt in a country lane with a flat back tyre. She had got out and was about to unstrap the spare wheel when a voice asked, 'Can I help?'

She had turned to see a thin, lank-haired man standing nearby. His shoes were badly scuffed and he looked as though he hadn't eaten for a week.

'I've got a flat tyre,' she said. 'You can change it, if you like.'

'Will do. Got a jack?'

'In the back. I'll get it. Don't be surprised if Mandy barks at you the whole time. She doesn't like strangers and men in particular.'

But the dog hadn't barked once and when he went to return the jack to the back of the car she edged forward to sniff his hand.

'Extraordinary,' said Victoria. 'I've never known her to be like that before.'

'Maybe it's because she knows I love animals. Dogs can tell.'

'You're right,' Victoria agreed. 'You've had pets of your own?'

He lowered his head. 'I did have. But my dog was put down by someone when I had to go away for a spell.'

Compassion for a fellow human being was a rare experience for Victoria but she felt its stirrings as she saw tears in the man's eyes.

'You must let me give you something for helping me out,' she said, reaching for her handbag.

He shook his head. 'That's all right.'

'Come on. I'd like to.'

He hesitated. 'Well, I could do with a bit of grub . . . A cheese roll and a beer would go down a treat.'

Victoria gave him an intent look and with the bluntness which had lost her friends said, 'You've been in prison, haven't you?'

He nodded.

'Discharged? Out on parole? What?'

He shifted from foot to foot and mumbled rather than spoke when he said, 'Couldn't get parole. Made a break for it.'

'You're on the run?'

'No. Well, yes. Sort of.'

'You can't be "sort of". Either you're on the run or you're not.'

'That's right. I mean, yes.'

'What were you in prison for?'

She had to strain to catch his reply.

'Armed robbery.' His voice became agitated. 'But it was the others who carried the guns. I didn't. And I didn't know they was. Wouldn't have touched it if I had. Anyway, I was only a look-out. But I got done same as the rest. My brief was useless. Everyone says I should have got off light. First offence.'

'Who did you try to rob?'

'Bank. It was a bank job. But it was botched.' He began moving away. 'You won't tell no one you seen me,' he asked anxiously.

165

She shook her head. 'Mandy seems to like you and that's good enough for me. How long have you been on the run?'

'Four months.'

'How on earth have you managed to live?'

'Picked up odd jobs here and there.' He gave a shy smile 'Diggin'. Any rough work with no questions asked. Tree loppin'.'

Victoria stroked her chin thoughtfully, her fingers moving as though she was caressing an invisible beard. With her other hand she swung her bag which Steve watched as if mesmerised

At length she spoke. 'I haven't got any trees that need lopping but I do have kennels. My partner isn't too well and I could use an extra hand for a day or two. How does that strike you?'

'You mean? . . . Me? . . . Workin' with dogs?'

'It's noisy and smelly and you'd be doing the dirty work cleaning and sweeping. Mucking out.'

He looked like a man bemused. 'It sounds heaven,' he said. ' always wanted that sort of job.'

'Right. That settles it. Two days. That's all. Get in.'

She had opened the passenger side door.

Two days had now stretched into a year and five days and i was the happiest time of his life.

Up at six in the morning in all weathers, seven days a week and seldom off duty before nine in the evening, he became an invaluable member of the kennel. He knew little of the pas history of the two women except that their friendship date from the time that they'd slept next to each other in the dormitory of a girls' boarding school, and they knew little about him except that he'd had a tough childhood in London's Eas End in which he'd lost trust in human beings and discovered th only worthwhile relationships for him were with the so-calle lower creatures of the animal kingdom. Only once did he let sli that he'd been married for a short period.

But although he was completely content with life at th kennel it was not entirely free from worry. When he was oblige to accompany Victoria to the nearest town to help with carryin something heavy he felt once again all the fearful anxieties of a hunted man. His eyes would constantly scan streets and shops looking not only for any sign of a police presence but also for possible escape routes if he should be cornered unexpectedly.

The best time had been at Christmas when presents were exchanged and he had given the women carvings he'd made secretly and in his spare time from driftwood. For Victoria he'd carved a fair impression of a spaniel, and for Sylvia a representation of her favourite breed, a retriever. From them he received a transistor radio and a wrist-watch.

He looked at this watch when Victoria called him a good lad for agreeing to attend to the paddock fencing. 'Think I'll push off to bed,' he said. 'Good night all.'

Sylvia lifted her head and smiled. 'Good night, Steve.'

Victoria raised her whisky glass in a farewell gesture. 'Night, Steve.'

Usually he fell asleep within seconds of switching out the light. He was accustomed to the sound of dogs barking during the night, to the howling which started by one mournful animal would spread to others so that a canine chorus of baying filled the night with such dolorous cries that they seemed to be expressing the sorrows of all warm-blooded creatures. And when the dogs were quiet he was used to the other noises – creaks in the bungalow, the calls of night birds and foxes – and none of these kept him awake. But tonight his thoughts prevented sleep. These were not thoughts in constructed sequences and they were not balances struck by logic; rather, they were well-worn phrases which had in common the conflict between self-preservation and conscience.

So what if the kid had been snatched? She was stupid to let herself be chatted up by a stranger. Keep a low profile. None of my business. Live and let live. Anyway, maybe they was playin' a game. Kids sometimes screamed with pleasure. Look after number one. If you don't, nobody bloody will. Don't spoil a good thing. Lie low. Go to ground.

She could be safe and sound by now. Someone else saw the telly and tipped off the fuzz. Waste of time to tell what I saw . . . But I could describe the guy and his car. Poor kid. She might be suffering. Tortured. There are some right bastards around. Perverts . . .

Don't have to go to the soddin' police station. Could call from the box by the Three Feathers. It's out of the way. First thing. Give a description and ring off sharpish. Could say he looked like he might have form . . .

If he does have form they'd have his prints. And he must have left his prints on the Coke can. Should tell them about the can. But there are so many cans littered round they'd never find the right one . . .

Forget it. Forget the whole thing. Go to sleep . . .

But he didn't sleep. He tossed and turned all night thinking of how he could get the information to the police with no risk to himself. He didn't want to involve Victoria or Sylvia. It's all down to me, he thought. And then, as the first light of day filtered into his room, he hit on a solution. He would go down to the beach and, wearing gloves, would pick up the can and put it in a bag. He'd then go to a 'phone-box, put a call through to the police, describe the man and his car, tell them that a Coca-Cola can with the man's fingerprints would be left in the box by the Three Feathers, hang up and make a run for it.

He dressed hurriedly and jogged his way to the beach. As he had anticipated, nobody else was there. He scrambled down the small cliff and ran to the dune where he'd been lying when he'd heard voices. The can, red and white, with *Coke* down one side and *Coca-Cola* down the other, was lying where it had been thrown. Steve slipped on an old pair of gloves, unfolded a plastic carrier bag, and picked up the can which he placed in the bag with all the care of a man handling a live grenade. Then he knotted the top of the bag so that the can couldn't fall out.

He looked around. A light breeze riffled the long grasses and to the east the rim of the sun poked over the horizon like a red tongue thirsting for the sea. No time to lose. He began to jog hi way back, not retracing his steps because the call-box lay in a different direction. He ran across common land, through heather and gorse, and down a deserted lane until he came to a main road. It was here he might be seen during the last quarter mile to the call-box and so he crossed the road and burrowed through a hedge so that the far side of the hedge could shield him from being seen by a passing car.

A heavy lorry thundered past just as he reached the shelter of thick hawthorn. Pausing a few seconds to gain breath before making a dash along the edge of a ploughed field he felt his heart beating uncomfortably fast. And then, to his horror, he saw a man standing in the middle of the field. He remained stock-still, willing himself to merge into the blur of the hedge. It was a few seconds before he realised he was staring unblinkingly at a scarecrow.

Now or never. Clenching palms which were sweating inside gloves he began running. For the last few yards it was necessary to break cover to cross the pub's car park and get to the box. He surveyed the red-brick building and noted that curtains of all upstairs windows were drawn. No one was awake yet. He listened. Silence except for bird-song. No cars humming along the road. It was safe to run, tiptoe, to the call-box.

Inside the box he leafed through the local directory until he found the number of the police station. Then he took out some loose change and dialled.

A woman answered. She gave the name of the station and added, 'Can I help you?'

He cleared his throat. 'You better take this down quick. I'm not hangin' around. I got information on the guy who snatched Sandra Willingham.'

'May I have your name please?'

'No way. Get this down. He's about forty, five foot six or so, pale thin face, wearing grey jacket and trousers, green socks and sandals. They was drinking Coke. He threw the can away. I got it with me. It's got his prints on it. He looked like he might have form . . .'

169

'Just a moment, please. Could you . . .'

'No questions. I'm speakin' from the box by the Three Feathers. I'll leave the can in a bag in the box. Oh, and he was drivin' a red Cortina. Hope you get him and he gets life. Bastards like him should be castrated. I'm off.'

He slammed down the 'phone and after a quick check that no one was nearby he opened the door and slipped outside. The months he had spent on the run had taught him how to move with stealth and to use cover.

He was half-way home when he remembered his gloves. They had been left on top of the telephone directory. A wave of hot panic swept over him before he turned and doubled back. It was unlikely that anyone could trace him through the gloves but nothing must be left to chance. Luck was with him. The gloves were where he had left them, the car park was still empty and there was no traffic on the road.

When he walked through the back door of the bungalow he was greeted by Victoria. 'Steve! Where have you been?'

'Couldn't sleep. Went for a stroll. Sorry I've been so long. I'll start cleaning now.'

'Don't forget the fence. After breakfast.'

'I hadn't forgotten. Will do.'

She gave him a searching look. 'Everything all right?'

'Right as rain, thanks.'

'You look as though you've been pulled through a hedge backwards.'

His nerves were taut but he had to smile inwardly, the sort of smile which begins in the mind but is monitored and erased before it reaches the lips, because she was right. He had been through a hedge, backwards.

'And you haven't shaved,' she observed. 'You look a mess. But men always are grubby one way or another. Nothing personal, Steve.'

'No. I understand.'

'I know you do. Most people don't though. They think I'm a hard cow.'

With this she turned on her heel and left.

Great, he thought. Mission accomplished. You bloody done it, Steve. For once in your life you done the right bloody thing.

He stepped jauntily to the cupboard where brooms and disinfectant were kept and before opening it executed a little dance. As he sloshed water down the stone passageway between kennels he began to whistle.

A highly-strung poodle began to howl softly at the sound of his whistle. 'Sorry, old girl,' he said. 'Didn't know we had a real musician with us. I'll stop.'

But inwardly he carried on whistling.

During the day he listened to newscasts on his radio in the hope that he'd hear an item about the missing girl but no mention was made of her. However, the newscaster on television in the evening said the police were still following leads although there had been a number of hoax calls.

'Hoax calls,' Victoria snorted. 'Whoever said the human race was a cancer on the face of the earth had got it right.'

'It's only a warped minority surely,' Sylvia murmured. 'What do you think, Steve?'

Until now he'd never sworn or used bad language in front of the women but in an outburst of anger he said, 'I'd bloody hang any bloody hoaxer. Straight I would.'

He went to bed, furious. Did the police think his call had been a hoax? Had all his nervous tensions and mental conflicts been for nothing?

He didn't have to wait long for an answer.

They came for him the following day.

It was half-way through the morning and he had just come back from exercising a dog in the paddock when a car arrived and two men in grey suits climbed out. He stood transfixed at the corner of a prefab which housed short stay dogs. He knew the fuzz when he saw it and the fuzz knew him.

'Just hold it there, Smith,' said one of the men.

Hold it! He was rooted to the ground. Paralysed. Dumb. How the hell had they found him? Someone must have shopped him. Said there was an escaped convict living at the kennel. But who?

Victoria came hurrying out of the back door. 'What's going on? Who are you?'

The first man flashed an identity card. 'Detective Sergeant Cook, madam.'

'And what do you want, might I enquire?'

Even in his paralysed state Steve was impressed by her intimidating and imperious hauteur. She wasn't afraid of the fuzz.

But the policeman was nonplussed. 'I want him,' he replied. 'Is he in your employ?'

'What if he is?'

'You knew he was a convict? An escaped convict?'

Speech and movement came back to Steve. He stepped forward. 'She don't know nothin' about me. Leave her out of it. I'm comin' quiet.'

He was shepherded into the back of the car where he sat with Detective Sergeant Cook while the other man took the wheel and drove the car down the rough road which led from the bungalow. Bewildered by the sudden turn of events it was a few moments before he articulated the question which burned in his mind.

'How the hell did you cotton on to me?'

Cook turned his head and gave a smile that was almost friendly. 'You were our informant about the Willingham girl, weren't you? Most helpful it was. Turned out he did have form, just as you said, and that made it easier for us.'

'What sort of form?'

'Assaults on minors. Child molesting.'

'Reckon you'll get him?'

'He's already been got,' replied Cook with satisfaction. 'We heard about it a few minutes before we came out here.'

'What about the girl?'

'Alive and unharmed, as far as we know.' The detective lifted his wrist and glanced down at the handcuffs. 'Sorry about these, but it has to be done by the book.'

Steve nodded. 'I know.'

'We owe you a vote of thanks.' Cook sighed heavily. 'Too bad you were careless. But you were, and we had to take you.'

The car turned on to a main road. Steve looked out of the window at other cars with free people inside. Did they appreciate how lucky they were to be free?

The car sped past the Three Feathers and the box from where he'd made the call. A flock of starlings was descending on the field; they were undeterred by the scarecrow which had scared him. Birds, like people in cars, were free to come and go as they pleased.

He was wishing he was a bird when by coincidence Cook said, 'How much bird had you got left when you scarpered?'

'Three months.'

'You were stupid to scarper. Three months wasn't much. Why did you do it?'

'It was my dog.'

'Your dog?'

'The wife was fed up with it. She was goin' to have it put down. She was divorcin' me, you see. She had it done the same day I got out. A bit earlier and I'd have saved him. And then . . . Well, I decided to stay out.'

The car glided smoothly past an articulated lorry.

'Not much further,' said Cook, breaking a long silence.

'You said I was careless. How did you cotton on to me?'

Cook grinned. 'Trade secret.'

'Was it someone? Did someone suss out who I was and tell you where I was livin'? Was I shopped?'

'No. You weren't shopped. You shopped yourself.'

The car slowed down as a speed-restriction sign came into view.

'We'd have got you one day anyway,' said Cook, 'so don't brood about it.'

But during the time before he appeared in court Steve tried hard to figure out what mistake he had made when reporting what he had seen on the sand-dunes. He had kept talk on the phone to a minimum and said nothing to reveal his identity. How had he been careless?

The question was still unanswered when he was led into the dock. Detective Sergeant Cook was the first witness to appear. He simply gave evidence of the arrest, not of the events leading up to it, but he did emphasise that the prisoner had offered no resistance and, indeed, had voluntarily given himself up to spare his employers any embarrassment.

Victoria was next to appear in the witness box. She spoke volubly and forcefully about his integrity, willingness to work, and kindness to all animals. His job would be kept open until he was free to return to the kennels. So far as she was concerned, he would always be welcome – 'more welcome than anyone else I can think of,' she added with a defiant look around the courtroom.

'I doubt if anyone would have the temerity to contradict you on that point,' murmured the judge.

The closing speech on Steve's behalf was made by an eminent Queen's Counsel whose services had been obtained by Sandra Willingham's father in gratitude for his daughter being found. Counsel argued persuasively. Was a man who escaped from prison for the sake of a dog's life, who had risked rearrest for the sake of a little girl's life – was this the sort of man who was a danger to society? Was this a man who deserved punishment?

In summing up the judge spoke of tempering justice with mercy and he took into account the public service rendered by reporting the abduction of a young girl. In the circumstances he would not impose any additional custodial sentence but the prisoner would have to return to jail to complete the original sentence less the amount of time he had spent in custody while on remand. Effectively this meant Steve would be free at the end of the following month.

Cook came to see him while he was in a cell waiting for transport.

'Just to wish you luck, Smith. And I hope we don't have to meet again. Professionally, that is.'

'Thanks.'

They shook hands.

'How did you get on to me,' asked Steve. 'Did someone in your lot recognise my voice?'

Cook shook his head. 'No reason why you shouldn't know. I was kidding when I said it was a trade secret. It wasn't your voice. It was your language. It was obvious when we ran back the tape. You talked of prints. You said the guy looked as though he had form. Ordinary members of the public don't recognise someone who looks as though he's got form. It takes one to know one, as they say. On top of that you came on strong about him being castrated. We all know what cons think of sex offenders, particularly offenders against kids.'

Steve frowned thoughtfully. 'I get that. But knowing I might have form doesn't mean nothing much. Hundreds could have it. Why did you think it was me?'

'Simple. If you did have form, as I suspected, and you left any clues in the box, I'd find out more about you. I decided to dust the box for prints. You may have worn gloves when you picked up the can but you weren't wearing them when you called us. You left a perfect set of prints on the instrument. It was lucky no one had used it in between.'

Steve sighed. 'So you knew it was me. But you still had to find me.'

'That was application. Solid application. It was short odds you must live in the area and it was a matter of getting someone in the locality to identify your photo. We came up with a milk delivery roundsman. He'd seen you once or twice on his rounds . . . Talking of rounds I must be on my way. All the best.'

As he moved towards the door Steve said, 'All the best to you too.'

Cook turned and grinned. 'I shall need it. I heard this morning I've got promotion and I'm down for a course at

Bramshill. Early promotion, as it happens. And do you know why?' His grin widened. 'According to the super it's because I've shown real form!'

David Williams

THE BULLY

'It's only the two of them, Alec. Worth a try. But you must go and see them. Honestly, it doesn't work otherwise.'

It was Robin's voice on the telephone. He sold insurance for a living so he knew what worked and what didn't. It was the second time he'd been on to me about recruiting people for Old Boys' Day at Petsford School. We had both been boarders at Petsford well over thirty years before.

'You know I've never been back before, Robin. Not once.' I'd already agreed to drive the two hundred miles across country from east Lincolnshire where I lived. Pressing others to do the same thing hadn't been part of the deal. Robin lived very close to Petsford. He had also recently been elected chairman of the Old Petsfordian' Society.

'Jordan and Yates haven't been back either. Not according to the records. All the more reason for getting them this year. You're setting the example. Funny they're the only Old Petsfordians in your area. And both our contemporaries. Makes it easier.'

'Not if you don't know their addresses.' And his other assertions had been only barely accurate. Robin was three years younger than me, making him forty-nine now. Windy Yates I reckoned to be fifty-three, and Touser Jordan would have been fifty-seven. So we were only contemporaries in the sense we'd all been at the school together for at the most one year. He'd hardly have known Yates, and Jordan probably not at all.

'We didn't have their *current* addresses.' Robin took up my point quickly. 'Have now. Pretty certainly. That's why I rang. Yates is a partner in Debit and Briggen, estate agents. Three offices round your area.' Then he gave me Windy's private address which he'd got from the telephone directory. I could have found it more easily. He implied as much, but quite tactfully. 'And there's a T. M. Jordan not that far from you. Inland a bit. Has to be the same one.' He supplied Jordan's address too. Robin had been busy since he'd rung me about the other two a few weeks earlier. Getting hold of a current Lincolnshire telephone directory couldn't have been that easy in Petsford. Obviously he'd rumbled I wasn't really going to make any effort tracing the others on my own. In the circumstances, I'd felt it important he should be seen to be the initiator.

I wondered again if I'd been right in getting involved – in agreeing to make the trip even. Of course I liked Robin. We'd kept up over the years. Not that we actually saw each other much. I'd bought a few small endowment policies through him. At different times he'd bought three of my pictures, and put several other buyers onto me – people interested in watercolours of wildfowl. That was it. He knew I owed him more than he owed me. Supporting him over what he called the rehabilitation of the Old Petsfordian Society under his chairmanship looked like a way of paying him back.

I telephoned Windy the night before going to see him. He lived nearly thirty miles from me: Peterborough direction. I had business pending with one of the galleries in the city anyway, so it didn't mean a special journey. It was his wife who answered. She sounded friendly enough, but when I explained why I wanted a word with Windy – Wyndham as she called him – she wasn't very encouraging.

'You sure you've got the right Yates?' she asked. 'He's W. I. D. Yates.'

'If there's another it'll be quite a coincidence, don't you think?' I said. 'Anyway, if he was at Petsford . . .'

'That's the point,' she cut in. 'I've never heard him mention it.' She paused, obviously perplexed. She'd known my name, and – more to the point probably – my work as well. I wasn't someone she wanted to snub. Well, something had to account for the respect afforded after I introduced myself. 'Look, he's out this evening, but he'll be here in the morning. If you want to drop by early. He's supposed to be taking me into town about ten.' But the tone implied they could hang on after that if necessary. I said it wouldn't be. She gave me directions on how to find them.

I thought I understood why Windy had never told his wife he'd been at Petsford. I was right, too.

The house was a bit stark – newish, in the 'Georgian manner', and all by itself in the corner of a field, with not much done to develop a garden. The village was half a mile away. Inside it was better – soft colours and nice bits of furniture, some of which really were Georgian.

Windy had hardly changed. He still looked undernourished. The normal expression on the thin, V-shaped face hovered somewhere between apology and fright. He had kept most of the wavy, sand coloured hair. His narrow chest went in where it should have gone out. 'Woe . . . woe . . . won't you sit down?' he asked. And he still had the speech impediment.

'It's been a long time. I'd have recognised you anywhere though,' I said.

'Would you like some coffee?' asked Mrs Yates. I accepted and she went out to make it. The shy little three-year-old went with her. Windy's wife was a good deal younger than he was, and quite a looker – a tallish blonde with nice legs, a short skirt and a confident manner.

'We knew each other at Petsford?' It was definitely a question and not a statement. Windy affected to have no memory of me.

'You were a year ahead of me. But we used to have art lessons together.' Art had been a voluntary activity.

He shrugged. 'Afraid I don't remember.'

'And we took up squash at the same time, too. Because we figured it was the only manly sport at which you couldn't possibly get hurt.'

I laughed at my own joke because Windy didn't seem to find it funny – not any more.

We had been very close friends before he had been withdrawn from the school. It was difficult to refer to what had really bound us together. We had both been badly bullied – subjected to what was euphemistically referred to as ragging. A lot of that had gone on at Petsford in our time – mental and physical persecution of a particularly vicious kind. I hadn't complained: just suffered, and plotted revenge.

'It's a period in my life I've tried to wash from my mind, com . . . com . . . completely,' he said, without emotion.

I could understand – even to the point of his not recognising me. In the end the persecutors had gone too far with Windy. There'd been a scandal after he'd 'told' on his tormentors following an initiation ceremony – another euphemism for a particularly sadistic and dangerous bit of dormitory horse-play. It had involved hanging the victim upside down from a window while his bare anatomy was subjected to various indignities.

Windy hadn't 'told' straight off. He'd run away from the school, been brought back by the police who'd found him weeping on a main road in the middle of the night, half-dressed and still terrified. It was then he'd been made to name those responsible. The curious thing was the ring-leaders got off with a beating from the headmaster: it was Windy who left the school – not kicked out, of course. His parents were advised his temperament wasn't suited to life in a boarding school.

The ragging had stopped for a bit after that – but not for long. I should know. The fact was the masters in general didn't have time or sympathy for weaklings. Windy had been the only victim ever to sneak, and the leader of the ragging happened to be a useful Rugby player as well as a sadist.

'You wouldn't be interested in driving over for Old Petsfordian Day? As my personal guest, perhaps? October 12th. It's a Saturday. We could go in my car. We'd need to spend the night. At the Red Dragon. The dinner's a formal affair . . .'

There had been no point in going on. He was looking at me in honest, blank amazement, shaking his head from side to side. 'I wouldn't go to that place as the per . . . per . . . personal guest of the Prin . . . Prin . . . Prince of Wales. Thank you very much Mr . . .'

He couldn't have forgotten my name again. It was nervousness. 'You used to call me Alec,' I said.

Then Mrs Yates came back, and we had the coffee. We didn't discuss Petsford any more, nor the Old Boys' Day.

It seemed Windy had married late – five years before. She'd been his secretary. He was enormously proud of her and the child. I had never married, and was mildly envious of both. The wife's hobby was painting. Thank heaven that provided a talking point. Otherwise the whole episode would just have been an embarrassment. Even so, I didn't stay long. I'd got what I came for.

As Windy showed me out, I asked with as much diffidence as I could muster: 'Ever come across T. M. Jordan? Touser Jordan? I gather he lives in the area.'

I swear he blanched – blanched perceptibly before recovering himself. 'Another local pay . . . pay . . . painter?' he enquired, trying to sound ingenuous.

'No. He was at school with us. I thought you'd remember him. One tends to recall chaps older than oneself. Not vice versa.'

But it was no use. Windy had steeled himself to recollect nothing. I admired the resolve. You see, Touser Jordan had been Windy's persecutor in chief: and mine.

It was some days later when I rang the doorbell at the Jordan bungalow. A drab little woman answered. She was probably about my own age but looked older – mousey hair pulled back in a bun, no make-up, and everything she was wearing seemed old, hand-knitted and a size too big. 'Come in, please,' she half whispered after I stated my business.

I hadn't telephoned in advance. I told her I'd been driving close by on my way home and dropped in on the off-chance.

The place had a run down look. It was clean and tidy, but it badly needed redecoration. The armchair I took seemed to have lost half its springs.

'You were a friend of my husband's?'

'We were at school together. Is he . . . ?'

She mumbled something I didn't hear properly. Then she repeated it. 'He died a year ago. Suicide.'

I heard that. 'I'm sorry. The telephone directory . . .'

'It was reprinted just before it happened. The new one will have my initials in it.' She was whispering again. I had to lean forward to catch the words. 'We were intending to move from here.' She was addressing the hands she was kneading in her lap, then she looked up. 'I was to have met him. At lunch time on the day. We were to see a flat. In a new block being built. On the coast.' She had raised her voice quite sharply – and deliberately, as if as a result of a decision.

I made to leave. 'I'm sure it's painful to . . .'

'No, I don't mind talking about it. In a way it helps. He was a manufacturer's representative. A salesman.' She paused.

'I see. Was he ill?'

'Worried, I suppose . . . that he was losing his grip. Possibly also his job.' But she didn't sound especially convinced about it.

'He was approaching retirement though?'

'In six years. If he'd kept his position. It was why he was intending to sell this house, and move to something smaller.'

'But you've stayed on?'

'I don't care for the coast.' She looked as if a sea wind would blow her away. But her wishes evidently wouldn't have influenced Touser. So he'd stayed a selfish bastard. 'And the

184

market for places of this type has dropped a good deal,' she added with dignity. 'Fortunately, I receive a pension. From his company. Death in service, you see.'

'Well, that's a blessing.' So she was evidently better off than they'd have been if he'd lived and been fired. 'It's still very sad for you.'

'Did you know my husband well?'

'We weren't close, no.'

'You didn't like him?' I didn't reply. 'I can tell you didn't like him. He made my life a misery. Is that a dreadful thing to say? To a stranger?'

'Not if it's the truth.' She'd started to cry.

'The thought of leaving here.' She shook her head. 'Where I have friends.'

'You mean when he was alive? To live in a flat . . .'

'An isolated flat.' She described the place. It happened I knew it: a concrete monster. It really was isolated – on a remote and pretty bit of coastland that should never have been built on anyway. 'I'd have gone crazy there. With him. Just him. You see he was so . . . so unkind to me. And so mean.'

'He might not have bought the flat.'

'Oh, he'd seemed quite determined. It was very cheap.'

'That building's still half empty, I believe. So it's not cheap enough even for . . .' I hesitated.

'Penniless failures?' She dabbed at her cheeks with a screwed up tissue. 'I believe he was thinking that when . . . It's where he killed himself. Threw himself off the roof. It's a flat roof. Four floors.' She'd gone back to mumbling.

'You weren't there?'

She shook her head. 'Supposed to be. Then he cancelled. I was to have taken the bus. Two buses. From here. Then, just when I was leaving, the estate agents rang. My husband had rung them, cancelling the appointment to view.'

'And he got the agents to let you know.'

'But my husband went after all. Except he couldn't see the flat. He didn't have a key. You'd need a key,' she enlarged, raising her voice slightly when I indicated I wasn't hearing her too well. She'd stopped crying.

'He got onto the roof.'

'There's a fire escape stairs. At the back. He used that. It was a Saturday. In February. Builders don't work on Saturdays. They didn't find him till next day. Somebody noticed the car.'

And she hadn't put out a hue and cry, or she'd have said so. How she must have hated him. Why did women stay with men they loathed? 'The estate agents were?'

'Debit and Briggen.'

I needn't have asked, of course. 'You were dealing with a Mr Yates.'

'I'm not sure,' she said – as though I'd put a question. 'It may have been. Somebody from there was at the inquest. A young woman. To confirm about the 'phone calls.'

They say vengeance is sweet. It seemed to me the sweeter for the maturing; the savouring. It would only have soured if he'd been happily married. What if I'd been facing a widow still prostrate with grief? It was a question that had concerned me. This confrontation had been the first opportunity to get the answer without arousing anyone's suspicions. So Touser had done a bit of good in his ending – perhaps for the only time in his life, if not as purposefully as his wife imagined.

She was a broken spirit. You could see that. And no doubt he'd done the breaking. But instead of having to go on enduring life with him, probably jobless and cut off, she was where she wanted to be. The pension was no doubt adequate. I looked about the room: had she just got into the way of being frugal? I thought so. Would the spirit heal? I thought it would. I'm used to studying faces. I do some portraiture. The tears had been from shame not grief: shame for not being grieved. The convention demanded sorrow.

'We'll never know if he went there planning suicide.' Her tone was now strangely matter-of-fact.

'He must have gone for some reason.'

186

'I thought probably because he'd changed his mind again. About wanting to see over the flat. But it was too late to ring the agency. They closed at one.' She shrugged. 'Then when he got there, depression must have overtaken him.' But again her words sounded highly speculative.

'I expect that was it. The coroner . . .'

'Decided the balance of his mind was disturbed. When he did it.'

I didn't stay for the tea she offered me.

One 'phone call, that's all it had taken to set the scene for murder. When Windy was out, a man purporting to be Touser rings the agency cancelling the appointment to view, and telling the girl there to call Mrs Jordan. Disguising one's voice is easy: imitating someone else's isn't, but that was unnecessary. The rest of the plan was plain sailing – deserted building site and a spot no one goes near in mid-winter. You could almost write the script without being there.

'There'll be a marvellous view from the roof, Touser.'

'Even on a day like this?'

'Come up and see.'

Any weakling could have pushed him over when he was off balance, gazing out to sea. There'd be no guard rail – there still isn't: I've been to see. His wife believing Touser had been depressed had fitted nicely into the scenario.

Windy had taken a risk pretending he didn't remember Touser. I mean it wouldn't have taken much for someone to unearth that they were at school together.

Touser might not have remembered Windy. As I'd said, it could have been a case of an older schoolboy not recalling a younger one – like Windy not remembering me, though I had big doubts about that too. What was downright inconceivable was Windy being able to wash Touser from his mind – ever: not Touser, of all people.

And it was Windy that Touser had dealt with at Debit & Briggen: I'd found that out, though it hadn't been in the local newspaper report of the inquest. I'd read that account very carefully. The whole thing had been a chance in a million – but an impulse worth indulging: still a risk worth taking.

Windy was safe in the way he'd chosen to play his hand: no problems there. It would have been interesting to have seen inside his mind when I turned up. He'd had the night to think about it, of course, but he'd shown himself a good deal more decisive than he'd been as a boy.

The contented widow was a sort of bonus, if you follow me: no pause for recrimination in that quarter. Pretty predictable, too, when you considered it. How could Touser have made life anything but a misery for someone close to him? I wondered if Windy had checked that out: probably not. On instinct he'd have come to the same conclusion as me.

What Windy couldn't have known was that I came face to face with Touser at ten that morning, in a car park. My first inclination had been to ignore the swine. He hadn't recognised me – not until I changed my mind and spoke to him. Then he was all over me. It was as if we'd been closer than brothers. He'd been as insensitive as ever.

Touser had told me about the arrangements, and pressed me to meet him again later, with his wife: to do them a favour: to give them my opinion on the flat, because I was local. He didn't remark on my still having the limp. That was understandable: it was he who'd permanently dislocated my leg all those years ago. I never 'told' about the ragging: said at the time I'd fallen down the dormitory stairs.

Touser did one thing that I savour still. As we were parting in that car park, I'd found I had no small change. I told him I'd have to telephone someone if I was to be at the flat at one. He'd gladly lent me 10p. It was the coin I'd used to call the estate agents.